CUTTING I...

"How about a little p... ...ye Fargo asked the soldier guar... ...im.

"Do your thing and shut up," the trooper snarled.

Fargo stepped close to the latrine and let his right hand slip down to his calf holster. He drew the knife out, and whirled around to send the thin blade through the air. The soldier gave a cry of pain and let his rifle drop.

Fargo swiftly pushed the barrel into the soldier's belly as the man stared at the thin blade imbedded in his hand. The Trailsman pulled the knife free. "Wrap your kerchief around that hand," he said. "You'll be fine when they find you in the morning."

"Damn you. You'll never get away with this," the trooper rasped through his pain.

But that was exactly what Skye Fargo meant to do—or else die trying . . .

THE TRAILSMAN 82

MESCALERO
MASK

by

Jon Sharpe

Ⓙ
A SIGNET BOOK

NEW AMERICAN LIBRARY

PUBLISHED BY
PENGUIN BOOKS CANADA LIMITED

NAL BOOKS ARE AVAILABLE AT QUANTITY DISCOUNTS WHEN
USED TO PROMOTE PRODUCTS OR SERVICES. FOR INFORMATION
PLEASE WRITE TO PREMIUM MARKETING DIVISION,
NEW AMERICAN LIBRARY, 1633 BROADWAY,
NEW YORK, NEW YORK 10019

First Printing, October 1988

2   3   4   5   6   7   8   9

 SIGNET TRADEMARK REG. U.S. PAT. OFF. AND FOREIGN COUNTRIES
REGISTERED TRADEMARK — MARCA REGISTRADA
HECHO EN WINNIPEG, CANADA

SIGNET, SIGNET CLASSIC, MENTOR, ONYX, PLUME,
MERIDIAN and NAL BOOKS are published in Canada by Penguin
Books Canada Limited, 2801 John Street, Markham, Ontario,
Canada L3R 1B4
PRINTED IN CANADA
COVER PRINTED IN U.S.A.

The Trailsman

Beginnings . . . they bend the tree and they mark the man. Skye Fargo was born when he was eighteen. Terror was his midwife, vengeance his first cry. Killing spawned Skye Fargo, ruthless, cold-blooded murder. Out of the acrid smoke of gunpowder still hanging in the air, he rose, cried out a promise never forgotten.

The Trailsman they began to call him all across the West: searcher, scout, hunter, the man who could see where others only looked, his skills for hire but not his soul, the man who lived each day to the fullest, yet trailed each tomorrow. Skye Fargo, the Trailsman, the seeker who could take the wildness of a land and the wanting of a woman and make them his own.

*1861, where the Pecos flowed
from New Mexico into Texas with the
blood of dreamers and fools,
good men and bad . . .*

1

The long, powerfully built bronzed figure lay flattened on the rock, clad only in a breechclout. His long jet-black hair was held in place by a Mescalero brow band, and his eyes were narrowed to little more than slits as he peered at the three blue-clad cavalry troopers sitting quietly atop their mounts. The soldiers, their yellow-gold scarves bright under the hot sun, were positioned on a ledge that commanded a sweeping view of the terrain. The near-naked figure half-rose, a tight smile edging his lips. He had already taken note of the other three troopers similarly positioned a quarter of a mile to the west, and knew there were another three a quarter-mile to the east.

They had all been put in place. The chief of the soldiers at the fort had a plan, and the big man's lips curled with disdain. He stood straight, the sun glistening on his bronzed skin as he faded back into the crevices of the rock formation to his rear. The pinto he had closeted there gave a quick snort as he approached. He climbed onto the horse and felt the warmth of the animal's hide against his thighs. He circled slowly down through the rocks, skirting sandstone pinnacles, and when he reached the flat ground where the three troopers would see him, he put the pinto into an easy gallop.

It took only moments for two of the three troopers to wheel their sturdy, red-brown army mounts, leave the ledge, and race down after him while the third one stayed in place. They would sweep in behind him and try to chase him into the area covered by the next three troopers. Once there, two of those three would race down to join the chase. He had seen them attempt the maneuver before, and he snorted in contempt as he raced on. The other times, other Mescalero had quickly turned away and fled and left the soldiers thinking their tactics had succeeded. This time he would show them better, the hard way.

Glancing back, he saw the two troopers had reached the flat land and turned to give chase. He made a sharp, swerving dash into the jagged sandstone rocks that rose high on his left, and kept the horse running hard through the narrow, twisting passage. The two troopers would follow, of course, but they'd have to go single-file after him through the narrow passage. He spurred the pinto forward. When he saw the high rock ledge appear, he rose, stood on the horse's back, and gave the animal an extra push with his feet as he leapt upward. His fingers clung and found a grip. He pulled himself up on the rock, instantly swung around on his stomach to lie flat on the ledge.

The two troopers came into sight, one a few yards ahead of the other, chasing the sound of the pinto as it ran on through the passage. The Mescalero let the first trooper race by, half-rose, and measured distance as he gathered his muscular body. He held another moment, poised, and when the second trooper passed directly below, he leapt through the air, like a bronzed lance of flesh and blood. He hit the trooper across the back, and clung there as the soldier toppled from his racing horse. He was still atop the man as he hit the ground hard. The soldier lay still. The tall, bronzed figure rose, turned the trooper on his side to see a young, unlined face, stunned into unconsciousness but very much alive.

The Mescalero rose quickly. By now the soldier's companion had found the pinto, and he'd have turned in the narrow passage and be charging back. The thought had barely flashed through his mind when he heard hoofbeats racing down the passage. Moving on quick, lithe steps, the Mescalero went to the trooper's mount and drew the rifle from the saddle holster, a standard army-issue Remington. He was waiting just in back of the horse when the other soldier raced into view and had to pull back sharply to avoid crashing into the first horse. When he recovered from his surprise, he found himself staring into the barrel of the rifle. He swallowed hard and the Indian's gesture was clear enough. The soldier swung down from his horse, and at another gesture from the powerful, near-naked figure, he turned around.

The sharp blow was just hard enough to send him crumpling to the ground. With a harsh sound the Mescalero tossed the rifle onto the trooper's unconscious form. He hurried up the passage, retrieved the pinto, and swung onto the animal's bare back. He brought the two army mounts back down through the passage with him, kept hold of their reins as he started across the flat land. He rode at a trot until he reached the place where the next three soldiers were in position to watch over another section of the land.

When the Mescalero caught sight of the three cavalrymen atop their place of observation, he spurred the pinto into a gallop and pulled the two army mounts along behind. He made a wide swing as he raced with the two riderless army horses and saw the three soldiers straighten up in their saddles. Two instantly swung their horses into action and began to race down after him. But he continued his wide swing, which brought him around to the rear of the rocks, and he suddenly swerved into a passage amid the sandstone. He halted, dropped the reins, and let the two army horses come to a stop. He left the mounts at the mouth of the passage and raced the pinto upwards. He was deep into the rocks before the two troopers halted at the horses.

He moved quickly through the rocks, swerved from one short passage to another until he yanked the pinto to a halt and leapt from the horse. He climbed on foot through the small spaces between the rock and came out a dozen yards behind the third soldier. The man's attention was riveted on the land below, searching for the two troopers who had gone in pursuit. The tall, bronzed figure moved noiselessly across the open space, long arms swinging loosely. The trooper neither heard nor sensed him until an arm came up, yanked him from the saddle, and circled his neck. He managed to utter only a strangled gasp until his breath shut off and he slumped to the ground unconscious. The Mescalero's black hair swung from side to side as he scrambled back across the rocks and returned to the pinto. He rode the horse higher into the rocks until he reached a place that let him look back and down. He halted, waited, and saw the other two troopers find the third one still unconscious on the ground.

He stayed, his eyes narrowed, watched the two troopers revive the third one. Slowly all three made their way down through the passages and pulled the two riderless mounts along. They disappeared from view as they wound their way downward and came into sight again when they reached the flat land. He saw them turn back and slowly begin searching for the soldiers that belonged to the riderless mounts. A grim smile edging his lips, the near-naked figure rode slowly down the back side of the sandstone formations. The six troopers would return to the fort bruised and battered and more than a little grateful they still lived. He rode in a long circle, sent the pinto up a low rise to ride parallel to a long line of shadbush that covered most of the rise. He edged closer to the trees, slowed as he caught the movement inside the brush, and quickly turned the pinto into the shadbush. The foliage moved again some twenty yards ahead of where he had stopped, and his eyes narrowed as he saw the horsemen appear, halt at the edge of the trees. Six, he counted, all Mescalero, all wearing brow bands and gray, loose-sleeved shirts, some with cut-down Levi's, others bare-legged. All were smaller than he, lighter, and narrower in the shoulder, each man with coal-black eyes, high cheekboned faces with hawklike features.

They were concentrating on a low hill and suddenly a rider came into view, a young woman with long, flowing hair the color of dry wheat. She rode an army horse and then, riding discreetly behind, at least twenty-five yards back, four troopers came into view. The girl rode well, her legs clad in riding britches, a dark-blue shirt covering breasts that swayed more than bounced.

The figure on the pinto watched as the six Mescalero moved their short-legged ponies, four fading back into the trees and hurrying in a half-circle while the other two slowly started toward the girl. He watched with his face growing tight, certain of what was going to happen and unable to prevent it. The two riders ahead of him stayed, let the girl draw closer, and then, with a sudden whoop and cry, they burst into the open and raced toward her.

The big man watched the four troopers instantly spur their horses forward as the girl slowed. They went into a full charge, swerved as one to intercept the two Mescalero. He knew that they thought the two Indians had failed to see them or were incredibly stupid. Their attention fully on the two Mescalero, they didn't even glance behind them as the four fast-racing Indian ponies swept out of the shadbush. When the troopers suddenly realized they were being trapped, a volley of arrows had already cleaved the air and the first two Indians had wheeled their ponies to attack from the front. He saw two of the troopers go down with the first hail of arrows, then a third. The fourth soldier tried to race toward the girl, but the two Mescalero cut him off. He had his rifle up and fired. One of the attackers fell from his pony.

The soldier tried to put himself between the Indians and the girl, but three arrows hurtled into him and he fell backward from his horse. He hit the ground but, in a final display of discipline, managed to empty his gun and send the nearest attacker toppling from his pony. The girl tried to flee and lost valuable time trying to dodge and swerve. Two of the Mescalero came up alongside her, yanked her from the saddle, and she landed on the ground hard. She lay still for a moment, then rolled, shook the dry-wheat hair, and pushed to her feet. The four remaining Mescalero brought their ponies in a half-circle around her and began to herd her forward. She turned and walked on as they rode alongside and behind her, pushing her into the trees.

The girl walked proudly, defiantly, and the tall figure on the pinto remained motionless in the trees as he watched. He wouldn't leave her to those four. They were scavengers—rotten, thieving scavengers. His right hand touched the handle of the thin double-edged knife in the waistband of his breechclout. The four moved into the trees with the girl and he slowly began to follow. He'd have to choose the one right moment he knew. He'd have but one chance. He stayed back. He had no need to see the four attackers and their captive. He could hear them as they moved through the woods, voices raised to exchange gruff grunts. They'd moved a few hundred yards when they suddenly stopped, and he heard a sharp cry of pain from the girl.

He slid from the pinto and hurried forward on silent, mountain cat's steps until they came in sight through the trees. They had dismounted and two had held the girl while the other two faced her. One, taller than the others with mean, twisted lips, laughed as he slapped her across the face. Her head snapped around at the blow, the dry-wheat hair swirling, but she brought her eyes back to him and refused to show anything but defiance. He could see her properly for the first time: the hair, shoulder-length and framing a face of finely molded features; a thin, straight nose; fine, slightly thin lips; and eyebrows that arched upward over light-gray eyes.

He moved closer as the mean-mouthed one reached forward, stretched an arm out, and his hand closed around the neck of the dark-blue shirt. He pulled downward, the garment ripped, and cream-white breasts flashed into the open for an instant.

But the girl twisted, tore away from her captors, and aimed a kick at the mean-mouthed one that caught him high on one leg. She tried to run but a hand seized hold of her hair. She cried out in pain as she was flung to the ground. Two of the men pounced on her while the tallest one fell to his knees as he straddled her twisting body. He started to pull the riding britches open. All four now had their backs to the big man in the trees.

He took a long, silent step forward, the double-edged blade in his hand, and was almost upon the four men when one turned, suddenly sensing danger. The man's hand flew to the tomahawk at his waist, but the sharp, thin blade came down in a sideways arc and his head almost fell from his neck. He collapsed as the line of red poured from his throat. The big man whirled, plunged the blade deep into the side of the tall, twisted-mouthed attacker as the man started to turn in surprise. The man's mouth came open as he staggered sideways and fell to the ground, his hand futilely trying to pull the blade from his side. But the other two had leapt up from the girl and came at him. One yanked a tomahawk from his waist, paused to take aim, and sent the short-handled ax hurtling through the air. The big man, with time to see the maneuver, waited a split second before dropping low, and the weapon sailed over his head. But he had to twist away from the charging second attacker and he felt the man's hands brush his shoulders. He kicked out with one foot, caught the Indian on the one knee, and the man went down with a grunt of pain. The big man whirled, and leapt forward. He brought his knee up hard, smashed it against the man's jaw, and the attacker's head snapped upward as he fell over in a backward arc.

The last attacker hurtled at him, a bone-scraping knife with jagged teeth held high. As the man came down with the knife, the near-naked, powerful form dived downward under the blow, slammed into the attacker's ankles, and the man did a somersault as his feet went out from under him and he catapulted forward. He hit the ground, the breath knocked out of him for a moment, tried to rise, and had time only to see the pile-driver blow smash down into his face. He gave a half-cry, half-grunt as it landed, then he shuddered for an instant and lay still.

The big man whirled, saw the girl starting to run, and cut her off in a half-dozen long-legged strides.

She stopped, her light-gray eyes narrowing at him. "You're one of them. Why'd you stop them?" she asked. "You just want me all to yourself? Is that it?"

He stared at the strong yet delicate loveliness of her. She had taken a moment to tie the torn pieces of the blue shirt together so that only the top, curving beauty of her creamy breasts showed. She stepped back as he said nothing, her eyes still narrowed, and he caught the tiny, despairing snort that fell from her lips.

"What's the use. You don't understand a thing I've said," she murmured and took another step backward.

He saw her eyes flick to a length of stout branch that lay broken on the ground. She edged closer to it and he moved toward her. She halted, waited, and with a fury and quickness that failed to surprise him, she scooped the length of wood up in her hand and swung it at him.

The near-naked man ducked, felt the club brush his hair, and he lifted a short left uppercut that landed on the point of her lovely chin. She went down at once, eyes snapping closed. He stood over her and admired the smooth swell of one longish breast that all but fell from the torn and knotted shirt. He reached down, tore off another piece of her shirt-tail, and made a gag for her mouth. She had a belt around her riding britches, and he took it off and tied her hands behind her back before he sat her against a tree trunk. He lowered himself to the ground across from her and waited until she came around, pulled her eyes open, and stared at him over the gag around her mouth. He rose, pulled her to her feet without anger, and led her to where the pinto waited in the woods. He sat her on the horse, swung on behind her, and felt the soft warmth of her rear against his groin. He rode slowly, unhurriedly and she turned to look up at him, a frown of incomprehension in her face.

He went up into the thick shadbush, swung north, and found a place that let him sweep the terrain below. It'd take time for the troopers he had toyed with to find their way back to the fort, and he guessed the day would be nearing an end before the chief of the soldiers sent his squads racing out to search for the girl. It would be a useless excursion, of course, and he almost smiled as he slid from the horse and lifted her to the ground. He sat down and pulled her to the ground beside him, his face impassive as he ignored the frowning stares she continued to turn at him.

The sun had begun to slide in the afternoon sky when he saw the spirals of dust rise in the distance. Soon the soldiers came into view. Two full squads, he saw, one racing east, the other west. They would find the four troopers who had been slain, of course, but the remainder of their wild forays would bring them only sweat and anger.

The big man strained his eyes at the nearest squad, but he couldn't be certain if it was led by the chief of the soldiers himself. Finally the racing horses disappeared from view and the sun went below the horizon. He remained motionless until the moon came up high in the night sky. Finally he stood, lifted the girl to her feet again, and put her on the pinto with him. He saw the questioning in her eyes as he slowly rode from the trees and down onto the flat, open land. He turned the pinto south, and another hour passed before he saw shapes of the buildings of the town that edged out from one side of the fort. It was no great fort, he thought, its stockade walls only moderately high with no corner turrets. Yet it was reasonably strong and he knew the sentries would be posted along the front walls. He sent the horse into a wide circle behind the fort, where he edged into a stand of rock and black oak.

He was directly at the rear of the fort when he halted, took the girl by the arm, and let her slide to the ground. He pointed at the fort and she gazed up at him. Why? her eyes questioned, and he saw gratefulness and relief mixed with total incomprehension. He pointed to the fort again and she began to walk, took a few steps backing up, and then turned and half-ran toward the fort.

He waited till she turned the rear corner on her way to the front gate before he moved the pinto back in the trees and hurried silently away.

He allowed a smile to crease his face. She would have her answer soon enough.

2

The big man rode the magnificent black-and-white Ovaro across the dry land, his lake-blue eyes narrowed as he saw the small knot of black-clad figures on the side of a low hill. Three raised mounds of earth, each marked with a simple wood cross, formed a straight line on the hill. Partly out of curiosity, he steered his way toward the figures and counted three women, two men, and four children, along with a preacher in his high collar and minister's coat. The small group parted as they started downhill toward three buggies, and the preacher passed near him.

"Respects," the big man said, and touched his hat.

"Thank you, stranger," the preacher said as one of the men came up.

"What happened?" the big man on the Ovaro asked. "Mescalero," the preacher answered. "Killed Seth Smith and his family."

"The new major at the fort said he'd be putting a stop to this," the man chimed in. "Haven't seen much change yet."

"He's trying. These things take time. We shouldn't expect miracles, Ben," the preacher said with ministerial charity.

"Obliged," the big man said. He turned the Ovaro away and rode down the hill continuing his journey across the dry land. At a rock formation he turned and followed its edge to a road running south. Geckos and chuckwallas scurried across his path and he took note of the unshod tracks of Indian ponies on the road.

Finally the town took shape before him in the distance and, nestling beside it, the stockade walls of an army fort. The town was called Dry Lake, the fort Midland. Certainly no major installation, it sat like a horned lizard at the edge of a vast territory of rock and sand, cactus and scrubland. New Mexico lay just west and the Pecos flowed south into Texas almost within sight.

The big man reached the edge of the town and paused to peer down the main street. Dry Lake seemed busy enough, with rigs and buggies lined up by what was plainly the general store, and he saw at least two grain sheds farther on down the street.

But there'd be time enough to explore Dry Lake. He turned the Ovaro toward the open gate of Fort Midland. Two sentries watched him ride in from the catwalk atop the stockade walls. Inside the spacious front yard of the fort he paused to take in the long, low building that was obviously the men's barracks, the blacksmith stand in one corner of the yard, and stables and grain bins along the back wall. A regimental flag hung outside what had to be the commander's quarters, and he steered the horse toward it, came to a halt, and swung to the ground. He took a small cloth sack from the saddle horn and slung it around his wrist as the corporal at the door brought his rifle up smartly.

"Came to see Major Honegger," the big man said.

"The major's not seeing anyone right now," the soldier replied.

"He'll see me. Tell him it's about what happened yesterday," the big man said laconically.

The soldier's eyes widened before he hurried inside. He returned in moments, excitement in his face. "Go on in," he said.

The big man brushed past him, barely fitting under the top of the doorway, and found himself in a large office. A territory map was on the wall and in front of it were a wooden desk and two straight-backed chairs.

The man seated behind the desk rose to his feet. He wore a crisply pressed uniform, every button in place and shined. The big man saw black hair with only the sideburns gray, a long, thin nose and thin lips—a face that was handsome enough yet without any real strength. It was marked by an air of faint disdain.

"Who're you, mister?" the major barked.

"Name's Fargo . . . Skye Fargo. Some call me the Trailsman."

"What do you know about yesterday?" the officer said, but Fargo's eyes saw the figure that had come into an open doorway to the right, dry-wheat hair tumbling down against a deep-red shirt. Her smooth forehead held a furrow and in the light-gray eyes he saw a probing curiosity as she peered at him.

"You can talk, Fargo. This is my daughter, Donna. She was involved," the major said.

"I know."

The major frowned at him. "You know that six Mescalero killed the four troopers riding escort for

22

her and then took her captive?'' he asked, and Fargo nodded.

"Then another one came, killed the first six, and took her with him," Fargo said.

"Then at night he brought her back here and let her go. Damnedest thing," the major said.

Donna Honegger stepped into the room. "He was bigger, taller than the others, and he never said a word," she offered. "But there was something else, something in his face. I can't pin it down, but it was there."

Fargo took the small cloth sack, pulled the drawstring open, and spilled the contents on the desk. The thick black straight hair tumbled out first, then a small packet of berries, a brow band, and a breechclout. "There's the Mescalero who took you from the others," he said.

The girl stared at the objects on the desk.

Honegger found his voice first. "Is this some kind of bad joke, Fargo?" he thundered.

"That's the brow band he wore," Donna said. "I remember it."

"And that wig is his hair," Fargo said. "The packet holds juniper berries. Mixed with water and a touch of red clay, they make a bronze dye. The rest is all he wore."

The major stared at the objects but Donna Honegger turned to the big man and her light-gray eyes stared hard at him. "That was it," she said suddenly, words bursting from her. "It just came to me. It was his eyes. They weren't an Indian's eyes. They were blue, the same blue as yours." Fargo let a tiny smile touch his lips. "It was you," the girl breathed. "That Mescalero was you."

23

"You get the cigar, honey," Fargo said blandly. He turned to meet the major's gaze.

"You were masquerading as a Mescalero?" the major asked.

"For the last two weeks. You want to see through a bear's eyes, you become a bear, or as close as you can get to one," Fargo said. "You had some other troopers who came in with their tails between their legs. They were the lucky ones. They came back."

"The same six Mescalero attacked them," Major Honegger said.

"They say they saw six of them?" Fargo asked.

"No, they said they saw only one, but there had to be others," the officer said with a touch of pompousness.

"No others. Just one. Me. That's why they came back alive," Fargo said. "I'm sorry I couldn't save the other four."

"Just you?" the major said, and Fargo saw the desire not to believe him in his face.

"Any Mescalero could've done it," Fargo said.

"Goddammit, mister, what's the meaning of this?" Major Honegger exploded, full of righteous anger. "What in hell is this all about?"

"It's called an object lesson, a demonstration," Fargo said calmly. He saw Donna Honegger watching him carefully.

"Of what?" the major snapped.

"Of how stupid your plan is for keeping watch on the Mescalero," Fargo said, and saw the man's thin-nosed face redden.

"How dare you say a thing like that?"

"I didn't say it. I proved it," Fargo answered.

"You proved nothing, Fargo," Danton Honegger said, disdain back in his face. "You came here on purpose, to do exactly what you did. You managed to pull it off with a combination of concentrated effort and luck. It proves nothing."

Fargo snorted with derision and glanced at the young woman. She looked on, plainly taking in everything with more than casual interest, her light-gray eyes slightly narrowed. She was damned attractive, he decided, the dry-wheat hair stark against the dark-red blouse, her figure slender yet with enough curve to it to avoid angularness. The major's voice interrupted and he turned away from her.

"Who sent you here, Fargo?" Honegger growled.

"General Redfield," Fargo said.

A sneer quickly appeared on the major's face to cover his surprise. "I might have known. It's just more of the old boy's jealousy. He hates to see someone else succeed, especially someone without his years of grubby, sweaty, bloody field service," Honegger snorted.

"Never knew him to be that kind of man," Fargo said. "But that doesn't change things a damn bit. You've a hell of a lot to learn about the Mescalero if you're going to fight them."

"I don't expect to do that for long. I'm not staying in this hellhole any longer than I need to. It's not going to devour me. I'll use it as my ticket to a promotion."

"You invited a senator and journalists here to put on a show for them," Fargo said. "But what you really did was invite them to their own funerals."

"I've invited them to see how a real commander commands, to see how an officer of ability handles the Mescalero," the major pronounced.

Fargo let his brows lift in silent contempt and turned his glance to the young woman. "Nice meet-

25

ing you again." He smiled and gathered the objects up from the desk to toss them into the small sack.

"You're not going to go on with that masquerade, are you?" the major frowned.

"Don't plan to, but you never now," Fargo said. "I do plan to stick around some." He reached into his pocket and pulled out a letter and dropped it on the major's desk. The man saw the official U.S. Army seal on the envelope and picked it up at once. He pulled it open and read the letter aloud in a crisp, authoritarian voice.

"Major Danton Honegger, this will introduce Skye Fargo, the Trailsman. I have sent him to aid you in whatever way he can. Listen to him. He knows the Indian like few white men do. General Howard Redfield."

The major let the letter drop onto the desk, the gesture one of disdain. "You'll forgive me if I'm not very concerned over the general's advice. I'm the field commander here and he knows what that means. But do stay around. You'll be the one to learn something."

Fargo's smile held its own condescension and he started to turn away.

"I am grateful for your saving Donna, Fargo," the major added. "I'll not forget that."

"Good enough," Fargo said, and strolled out of the office. He had reached the Ovaro when Donna Honegger came out, the red shirt resting against tiny points as she stood very straight.

"Wait, please," she said. "Come back in the morning. I'd like to say my own thank yous."

"Why not?"

"Where are you going now?"

"Got some people and places to look up," he said.

She turned and hurried into the building without another word. She had some of her father's authoritarian manner, Fargo noted, but her face held strength where the major's held weakness.

The Trailsman swung onto the Ovaro and rode out of the fort, making a sharp turn left and starting down the main street of the town as the day drew to an end. Dry Lake was already closing down. Most of the buckboards were gone, the general store locked and shuttered. Long shadows edged the street. Most of the riders in the town seemed to be heading for the same spot Fargo was, and he reined up in front of the saloon to see an almost full hitching post. He dropped to the ground and strolled inside. Dance halls and saloons were always the best places to ferret out information. In every town across the land they were whiskey-soaked crossroads of gossip, and he was sure this one would be no different.

Inside the swinging door, he paused to scan the smoky room, the bar at one side with a dozen customers lounging against it, a handful of battered, round tables along the opposite wall. The four girls that sat at the tables were almost stupendously unattractive, each one more worn than the others.

Fargo walked to the end of the bar. "Bourbon," he said, and the bartender, a small man with black curly hair and a pencil-thin mustache, shrugged apologetically.

"No bourbon, *señor*," he said. "Whiskey?"

The whiskey was probably rotgut, Fargo told himself. "Tequila," he said, and the bartender quickly poured a drink, nodded in satisfaction. Fargo took a sip and agreed that it was indeed good tequila. "Looking for somebody," he said. "*Hombre* used to live around these parts. His real name was Miguel but he was called Pecosito."

The barkeep's eyes widened in recognition. "*Sí*, Pecosito. He comes in maybe once a month. He lives by Red Bluff Lake," the man said.

Fargo pulled on memory, his lips pursed. "Red Bluff Lake is right on the border," he said.

"Pecosito's place is on the Texas side."

"Obliged." Fargo nodded and tossed the man an extra coin as he finished the tequila and went outside into the night. He'd look for Pecosito in the morning with the help of daylight. He rode from town, passed the fort, and saw the gate was still open, two sentries standing guard. He slowed to a halt in front of the troopers. "Evening, friends." He smiled. "You keep the gate open all night?"

"Yes, sir, two sentries on four-hour shifts," the one soldier answered. "Major Honegger feels that leaving the gate open makes a statement to the Mescalero, letting them know he's not afraid of them."

"It makes a statement, all right. It says how damn dumb he is," Fargo answered, and both troopers shrugged uncomfortably.

Fargo moved on across the countryside, a red-orange half-moon high in the sky. He found a big bur oak and settled down under it for the night. He lay atop his bedroll, a parade of thoughts keeping sleep away, all centered on the meeting that had brought him here. Kansas, just south of the Cimarron, where he'd broken trail for Cy Allwin from Nebraska without their losing a hand to the Pawnees. He'd been relaxing in Meade when the two uniformed cavalrymen had found him. General Howard

Redfield had learned he was there, they told him. Fargo accompanied them to a field headquarters a dozen miles from the town. He remembered his smile when he saw the general standing even with a cane. "Last time you were still flat on your back with that hole in your leg," Fargo had said.

"I told you they couldn't keep a good man down," the general had said. His face echoed a lifetime of trails, of blood and sweat, of mountain and prairie. Fargo had worked for Howard Redfield before and knew there was no hollow ambition in the man, no falsity and no pretense, despite Major Honegger's accusations.

"Got a problem, Fargo, old friend," Redfield had said, easing himself into a chair in his tent. "Don't know that it can be solved, but maybe you can help. Down Mescalero way."

"Sounds uninviting already." Fargo grimaced.

"There's a Major Danton Honegger, a conceited ass with damn little ability and less common sense. He's field commander at Fort Midland, smack in the middle of Mescalero country," the general had said. "He was commanding the north Colorado territory until it all but exploded under him. They yanked him out and he wound up at Fort Midland. Everything done by Washington without my approval."

"Why?"

"You know the army. Hide your mistakes someplace else and hope they don't show again. Besides, he has friends in high places. He pulls strings that keep him untouched."

"Why don't you go down and take it over?" Fargo had questioned.

"Officially, I'm on the disabled list even though the entire region falls into my command," Redfield had said. "Honegger sent me a list of some of his plans for handling the Mescalero. I read them and got sick. One was to put out small groups of observors to keep overlapping areas under surveillance. What scares me most is that he's going to do real harm by making the settlers think he knows what he's doing."

"Giving them a false sense of security," Fargo had said.

"Exactly, and that'll be even worse for them. But now I've learned that a senator and a passal of journalists are going down to explore the territory under Honegger's protection. If these people are killed it'll be my neck that gets chopped off."

"Why for God's sake?"

"That's the way the army works. He's the field commander on the spot. He has the right to reject anything I say from here. But if he screws up, he doesn't fall alone. He's in my command and I'll take the heat, too. Seeing as how I can't get down there with this leg, I'm caught in a squeeze, like a man attending preparations for his own funeral."

"What do you figure I can do?" Fargo had asked.

"If you're down there, maybe you can find a way to get him to listen to good sense. I guess I'm asking you to try to find a way to keep him from turning bad into horrendous and horrendous into disaster," Redfield had admitted. Fargo had turned the words in his mind and waited in silence. "I know, you don't work for nothing," the general had added. "The usual special assignment pay." Fargo remained silent. "All right, double the usual."

"That's better," Fargo had said. He'd left after a shared drink, a few more reminiscences, and a handshake. He'd gone south, riding slowly, and formed his own plans as he rode. They were good plans, sharp and telling, and the surprise was still with him. He'd given Major Danton Honegger an object lesson he never expected him to dismiss. Yet he had done so, almost cavalierly. Honegger was more of an ass than Redfield had said, Fargo decided. He closed his eyes, pushing aside further thoughts to let sleep replenish mind and body alike.

The night remained still and he slept well. The sun was in the sky when he woke. He used his canteen to wash, breakfasted on some johnnycakes in his saddlebag, and finally led the Ovaro from under the oak. His gaze moved slowly across the spired and pinnacled rock formations forming a backdrop to the myriad of cactus, from the small mesquite to the giant saguaro. To the west, the Guadalupe Mountains rose, no towering awesome Rockies but with their own strength and sharp, jagged formations. He turned his gaze down across the lowland, a dry, flat mesa with an occasional trickling stream.

This was the land of the Mescalero, the people of the mescal, and like the cactus, as thorny and harsh and as capable of surviving where no other living thing could survive. The Spanish conquistadores had tried to conquer this branch of the Apache and failed. The French were next to try, and with the same results. Now the Mescalero fought another intruder who came back relentlessly, nesting, settling in, making conquest by intrusion and numbers. But the Mescalero fought back, as they had for centuries, and they used their own brand of ruthless tactics part Apache, part Aztec, part Spanish.

Fargo grimaced as he climbed onto the pinto and sent the horse toward Dry Lake and Fort Midland. He had ridden only halfway there when he saw the rider approaching, her dry-wheat hair glinting in the sunlight. She reined up when she reached him, and he saw she wore a white linen shirt that hugged the contours of her slightly long breasts, tucked in at the waist tightly to outline the two softly curved cups.

He fastened a glare at her. "Why are you out here alone? Do you just enjoy being captured?" he growled.

"Decided to come out to meet you," Donna Honegger said. "About yesterday, I'm more than grateful you were there. I wanted you to know that. Daddy can be so stiff-backed. Besides, I prefer to do my own talking."

"Always a good idea," Fargo said, and turned the Ovaro north.

"Where are you going this morning?"

"To find someone," Fargo said.

She came alongside him and he caught the hint of amusement in the sidelong glance she sent his way. "I'm trying to decide if you were more handsome as a Mescalero or as you are now," Donna Honegger said. "Of course, I saw a lot more of you as a Mescalero."

"We can fix that anytime you like, honey."

"I'm sure," she said with a hint of reproof.

"I'll circle south and see you back to the fort."

"No need. Daddy has his teams of observers back in place," the young woman said, and Fargo frowned.

"Again? He didn't learn enough yesterday?" he asked. "Damn the man's stupidity."

"I'll be quite safe going back, he told me," Donna said coldly.

"The way you were yesterday?"

"I went past the patrol points. That was my mistake."

"Listening to a damn fool was your mistake."

"You make hasty judgments, don't you?" she said with tartness.

"I don't need to eat a whole egg to know when it's bad. One mouthful will do."

"You ever think he was right about yesterday. Maybe you were lucky in pulling it off. That was your object; to show you could do it. That doesn't say the Mescalero will think that way," she said.

"All chicken hawks think the same way about a chicken," Fargo growled. He started to turn south but then reined to a halt. His lips pulled back and his eyes grew narrow as he spied the half-dozen slow-wheeling shapes in the distant sky.

"Buzzards," the girl said, following his eyes.

"Just about where he had the first team of observers yesterday," Fargo said. "Shit." He sent the Ovaro into a gallop. He didn't bother to glance back, but he heard her coming after him as he raced up the slow incline, across the top and headed toward the sandstone rocks.

Most of the buzzards had settled to the ground when he reached the rocks. He had slowed and Donna had finally caught up to him. His Colt in hand, Fargo moved forward carefully, solely out of prudence. He was too late to prevent anything. The presence of the buzzards proved that.

The Trailsman climbed through the rocks to reach a stretch of level stone higher amid the pinnacled formation, and the buzzards took flight as he rounded a tall slab of granite. He pulled to a halt and heard the curse drop from his lips as he grimaced.

"Oh, my God," he heard Donna gasp out as she

saw the three naked bodies on the ground. Their guns, belts and clothes had been taken, and the corpses had already been gouged by the buzzards. But the scavenger birds had done the least of it. The three troopers had been mutilated, one scalped, one raked down his chest and stomach by a hide scraper. The third one had had his genitals cut off. "Oh, God, I'm going to be sick," Donna breathed as Fargo swung to the ground.

He whirled at her, yanked her from the saddle, and slapped her sharply across the cheek. She blinked, instant anger leaping into her light-gray eyes.

"Now you're not going to be sick," Fargo said. "Stay here." She swallowed hard and waited by her horse as he stepped to the three naked bodies, knelt down, and carefully studied the ground around each, his eyes taking in the moccasin-clad footprints that covered the area. "Four, at least, maybe six," he murmured, and stood up, crossed to the Ovaro in three long strides, and swung onto the horse. "You know where he put the next three troopers today?" he asked Donna.

"North. He said he wanted to expand northward," she answered.

"Get back to the fort," Fargo said as he wheeled the Ovaro around.

"No, I'm going with you," Donna said, and from a deep pocket in her riding skirt she drew out a big six-shot, single-action Allen & Wheelock army revolver. "I know how to use it," she said. "I want to help."

He shrugged and put the pinto into a gallop. She was only a few lengths behind him as he left the rocks and rode hard along the flat ground. He'd no time to argue with her, and if this was her way of making up for her daddy's stupidity, he'd not deny it to her. He rode hard, sending the powerful horse flying across the dry dirt, steering to the right as he came in sight of the sandstone rocks that rose up from the flat floor. He caught the motion atop a ledge at the front edge of the rocks and started to push the Ovaro further.

"Stay back," he called over his shoulder.

"No," Donna Honegger shouted back.

"I won't be nursemaiding you," Fargo said.

"Don't expect you will," Donna returned.

He kept racing forward, sending his horse into the sandstone rocks and racing through a passage that led upward. He heard the shots, two, then two more, pistol shots. He swerved through a narrow gap and reached a level stretch. He saw the Mescalero first, at least four and on their horses. They were racing back and forth across a low fence of rock, and he saw two more shots come from behind the stones.

The Indians had attacked on horseback, plainly, and that was the only reason any of the three soldiers had been able to get behind the rocks alive. Two of the Mescalero heard him charging and tried to spin their mounts around. Both toppled from their mounts as the Colt barked twice. The Trailsman brought down a third one who started to turn, and the fourth Mescalero spinned, flattened himself across his pony, and escaped the shot. Fargo automatically flung himself off the Ovaro as a shot rang out from behind and above him, and he hit the ground as the bullet flung up slivers of dirt and rock only inches from his head. He rolled, spotted a crevice, and flung himself into it as another shot barely missed him and he spied the Mescalero on horseback a dozen feet higher into the rocks.

Fargo's glance went to Donna. He saw her rein up as the Mescalero in front of her charged. She fired as she leapt to the ground, emptying the six-gun. The Indian stayed flat on his pony to avoid the hail of bullets as he charged past her and raced on. Fargo lifted his Colt to fire at the Mescalero who had been in the high rocks, and he saw the tail of the Indian's horse disappear into the sandstone. He pushed himself to his feet, saw Donna stand up unhurt, and turned his attention to the troopers behind the row of low stones.

Two stood up, their young faces strained with shock. "Murphy's dead," one said.

"They sneak up on you?" Fargo asked, reloading his Colt before holstering the weapon.

"The one higher on the rocks had. We didn't know he was there. But the other four just came charging and we turned to face them. That's when he began to pick us off from higher up. We went behind the rocks. We didn't know how many more were up there," the soldier said.

"Take Trooper Murphy and go back to the fort," Fargo said.

"We ought to warn Henderson and the others. They're on duty south of us," the soldier said.

"It's too late for that," Fargo answered grimly.

"Aw, damn," the soldier murmured, and suddenly grew excited. "There's a third set of observers due west of here," he said.

Fargo glanced at Donna and saw the grimness in her lovely face. "I'll find them. You go back," he said. The troopers turned away and began to lift their slain comrade from behind the stones.

Fargo swung onto the Ovaro and saw Donna start after him as he returned to the flat land and turned west. "You did well back there," he said. "You didn't panic, but you don't have to go with me."

"I want to."

"You can't make good his mistakes." Fargo saw fire leap into the light-gray eyes.

"That's a rotten thing to say. I'm not doing that at all."

"The hell you're not," Fargo said. He sent the pinto into a fast canter. She caught up with him in moments, her eyes still afire.

"You've no right to say that," she said. "I'm coming because I think I can help, that's all."

"No sale, honey. And if you believe that, you've got problems."

"Meaning what?"

"You want to do right. You also want to protect Daddy. You're on a collision course with yourself," Fargo said harshly.

"Go to hell, Fargo!"

"You turning back?"

"No, dammit."

"Didn't think so." He laughed and returned his concentration to riding as he saw the red-clay rocks come into sight. He rode toward them, his eyes searching along the formation from left to right and back again. As he neared, Donna at his side, he spied the small open space halfway up the formation. The sun caught first the yellow kerchiefs, then the blue uniforms.

Fargo rode directly at the three cavalrymen and let them watch him take a passage up to the ledge. When he reached the three figures, he saw their eyes widen as they recognized Donna. In quick, terse sentences he told them what had happened to the other two teams and watched the nervous dismay take hold of their young faces. "We'll ride back to the fort with you," he said.

"Trooper Harrison, sir. You're saying we should just leave on our own?" a rangy young man asked.

"I sure as hell am, soldier. You're sitting ducks out here, just as the others were," Fargo said.

"That'd be against orders, sir. The major could have us dismissed or jailed for that. We're supposed to stay here till replacements come to take over," the soldier said.

"The major doesn't know what happened to the others this morning," Donna broke in. "I'll make him understand you did the right thing by returning to the fort."

Fargo watched the three soldiers exchange uncertain glances, their youth, discipline, and sense of duty fighting with the instinct for self-preservation. He sympathized with their dilemna and decided harshness would go further then understanding. "You've a choice. You can face the major or the Mescalero," he said. "You can be dismissed or you can be dead." He turned the Ovaro and spoke to Donna. "Let's go, honey."

She fell in beside him. He glanced back and kept the smile inside himself as he saw the troopers begin to follow.

They rode across the flat land toward town and the fort. Fargo's eyes swept the perimeter of the terrain as he talked to Donna riding alongside. "What are you doing out here at the fort?" he asked.

"Been with my father ever since Mother passed on some five years back," she said.

"Then you were in the north Colorado territory

with him." Fargo ventured, and saw the light-gray eyes narrow and her lips tighten for an instant.

"Yes, I was there," she answered, and the bland airiness of her voice didn't match the tightness in her face. He didn't press further. Besides, he had his answer. Daddy's obstinate stupidity wasn't new to her, yet she was too loyal to be anything but protective. He had to try to keep her from being one more problem.

"A man's entitled to one mistake," he said evenly.

She cast a quick glance his way. "Tolerance? How unexpected," she commented tartly.

"I try," he said, and saw more of the tightness leave her face. "The first two troopers are back by now, so our part of the story won't be a complete surprise."

"I think maybe you ought to let me handle my father," she offered.

"Why not?" Fargo said pleasantly, and drew another questioning glance.

"You've suddenly turned very agreeable," she said and he swore inwardly. She was too sharp. But she had grown friendlier and he wanted to keep it that way.

"I'm here to stop mistakes from getting out of hand. I'll take all the help I can get," he said, the answer honest enough, and she nodded acceptance as they rode into the fort.

Major Honegger was waiting in the doorway when they rode to a halt and dismounted. Fargo saw his eyes go to the three troopers following directly behind.

"Why are those men here? They'd no orders to leave their posts," the major said.

Fargo felt irritation flare inside him at the man's

officious pompousness. "We asked them to escort us back."

The major speared him with faint contempt. "You asking for an escort, Fargo? Hardly likely," Honegger sneered.

"It was my idea," Donna interjected quickly.

"Your idea?" her father echoed with an icy glance. "Since when are you in command of this post?"

Donna's lips tightened, but she held back hasty replies, Fargo saw with approval. "In view of what happened to the others it seemed only a matter of time before they'd be attacked," she said quietly.

"I hear Fargo's words coming out of your mouth, my dear," the major said.

"You hear what I saw with my own eyes." Donna shot a glance at Fargo. "Will you excuse me, please?" she said, and stormed into the major's quarters. The man followed and Fargo started to turn aside but not before he heard Donna's voice as she closed the door. "Dammit, Daddy, I'm trying to help you," she said. The closed door shut out anything further.

Fargo paused beside the three troopers, who had dismounted to wait with worry creasing their faces. "It'll be all right," he said, and hoped his reassurance would prove right. He led the Ovaro to the side of the yard and leaned against a hitching post to wait. It turned out to be a longer wait than he had expected, but the door finally opened and Donna came out, found him, and hurried over with a somewhat wry smile on her lips.

"I'm not very popular at the moment, but it's all taken care of. They'll get nothing more than a reprimand," she said.

"I'm sure you'll be popular with those three troopers," Fargo said. Her shrug held a kind of grateful acceptance. He turned and started to climb onto the Ovaro.

"Where are you going?" she asked.

"Where I started to go this morning, to find someone. I've enough daylight left."

"May I come along?" Donna asked, and he paused. "I don't feel like staying here at the moment," she added.

He continued to pause as thoughts collided inside him. He'd made her see things she didn't want to see, and he didn't want to push her back into being protective about the major. She'd been helpful and she could be helpful again if he could keep her eyes open to the truth.

"All right, come on."

"She hurried to her horse and rode from the fort beside him. He headed south, put the pinto into a smooth, ground-eating stride, and saw her handle the army mount well as she brought the horse into an almost matching stride.

"Where are we going?" she asked.

"To find an old acquaintance they call Pecosito," Fargo told her.

"Why?" Donna asked.

"Because he'll know about the Mescalero," Fargo said. "He'll know if things are normal or if they're on the warpath. He'll know who holds power and maybe a lot more."

"Why is that important to know?"

"I'm not sure but the more I know the better I'll feel."

"Because you think Daddy will do something

wrong," she said, and a trace of defensiveness colored her tone.

"Maybe," Fargo said, and realized she'd know it was a turn-away answer. He increased the Ovaro's stride and she had to concentrate on keeping up with him. He saw the sun starting to slide down toward the horizon when he came to Red Bluff Lake and slowed. He rode alongside its oblong contours and knew he had passed onto the Texas side of the border where the lake grew wider. He slowed and his eyes swept the terrain ahead where a stand of hawthorn edged toward the shoreline. He had reached the trees when, another hundred yards on, he spotted the round-roofed structure, unmistakable and unique.

"What's that?" Donna frowned.

"A wickiup. A framework of poles and branches covered with twigs, leaves, and grass," he said. "The Mescalero use both the tepee and the wickiup."

"The Mescalero? Is this Pecosito a Mescalero?" Donna asked.

"One-quarter Mescalero, three-quarters Mexican," Fargo answered. "Like a ferret, he managed to survive both sides of his ancestry." He rode to a halt in front of the structure, and the small figure emerged, a monkeylike body, short and wiry with thin arms and legs, all topped by a sharp face with long black hair and a somewhat beaked nose.

"I'll be the son of a three-legged mule. Fargo, by God!" Pecosito hurried forward on agile legs. "Long time since you come this way."

"Long time, Pecosito," Fargo said, and swung to the ground. He offered Donna a hand as she dismounted, and the small man peered at her with sharply appraising eyes.

42

"You bring your woman?" Pecosito asked.

"She wanted to come," Fargo said. "Her name is Donna."

The small man's eyes twinkled as his eyes continued to take in the young woman. "Donna," he echoed. "It means a lady. It fits the *señorita.*"

"Thank you." Donna smiled and Pecosito gestured to the wickiup and she followed Fargo inside.

"Place looks pretty much the same," Fargo said, taking in the fur pelts, the trading beads, the shiny baubles, and the jars of silver coins. "See you're still trading with the Mescalero."

"And any other tribes when they want. You know that is how I make a living, old friend," the little man said.

"I know. You make a living by always having something to furnish, something to exchange; sometimes beads, sometimes furs, sometimes information, sometimes gossip." Fargo smiled.

The little man eyed him with a cautious smile. "You have not come by for beads or pelts, I know, Fargo."

Fargo echoed the man's smile. "You know right, Pecosito. It has been a long time since I rode this land. There is a new commander at the Fort. I want to know what is new with the Mescalero."

"There is a new chief," Pecosito said. "He is very smart and very bad. He hates the *gringo* most but he hates almost everybody except his own people. He came up from the south, near the border. His name is Mangas Coronado but most call him just Coronado. He has many young Mescalero joining him."

"You hear if he has special plans?" Fargo saw Donna listening with fascination.

43

"To kill the white men," Pecosito said.

"There's nothing different about that. The Mescalero chiefs have been doing that a long time," Fargo said.

"That is true," Pecosito said, and frowned into space, his thoughts unspoken but plainly whirling around inside.

"What's poking at you, Pecosito?" Fargo asked.

"Nothing, maybe," the little man said.

"Something, maybe. Spit it out," Fargo pressed.

"I see things that do not fit, things I have never seen before. I see things that make me wonder," Pecosito said. "I see a soldier ride in the night. I see Mescalero warriors meet him and take him to the foothills of the Guadalupe where Coronado has his camp."

"The Mescalero talking to the soldiers?" Fargo said, and felt his own brow crease. "Dammed if I ever heard of that. You sure?"

"I saw it three times, late at night. I was hunting."

"Are you sure it was a soldier from the fort?" Donna cut in. "Maybe it was someone wearing part of a uniform."

"He came from the direction of the fort. He rode an army horse. He wore a full uniform," the little man said. "I followed one night and saw him ride into the Guadalupe."

"That's sure a new twist on things," Fargo said. He cast a glance at Donna and saw her frowning. "Got any ideas, old friend?"

Pecosito turned his hands up. "Nothing, nothing. It is like the wolf lying down with the sheep. I cannot understand it. I would not believe it if I had not seen it for myself."

"I know the Pueblo stop to trade with you. Have they said anything? Have you heard the wagging of loose tongues?" Fargo asked.

"Only what everyone knows, that Coronado is full of hate, for the soldiers especially," Pecosito said.

"But he talks with them in the dark of the night," Fargo murmured. "It doesn't add up at all."

"Because there's some kind of mistake here," Donna said crisply.

"No mistake, *señorita*. I know what I saw. Not once but three times," Pecosito said with a touch of affront in his voice.

"I know you do, old friend," Fargo said quickly, and put his arm around the little man's shoulders. "I'll come back soon. Meanwhile, I want you to keep watching and listening. Ask questions of anyone who comes by. I don't like what I hear."

"For you, Fargo," Pecosito said, and walked out of the wickiup with the big man.

"Nice to have met you," Donna said politely as she climbed onto her mount.

Pecosito executed a surprisingly courtly bow. Fargo waved as he rode away with Donna, who waited until they were moving along the shoreline before she spit out words. "Why are you so quick to believe anything that points a finger at Daddy or his men?" she accused.

"Why are you so touchy about it?" he threw back at her.

"I'm not," she snapped with a toss of the dry-wheat hair. "I just think your friend is either mistaken or he enjoys creating intrigue. It's probably the only way to add spice to his existence."

Fargo studied her for a moment. "That may not be the dumbest damn thing I've ever heard, but it sure comes close," he said, and realized the rapport he had taken pains to establish with her was fast unraveling. Maybe it wasn't worth the effort in the first place, he pondered. Grimacing inwardly, he spurred the pinto into a fast trot as dusk began to settle over the land.

Donna rode in silence beside him until they arrived back at the fort after the night had settled down.

"I'm sorry you can't keep an open mind," she said loftily as she handed her mount to a big, burly sergeant who stepped from the major's quarters. The man, square-jawed with a heavy face and small eyes under a close-cropped head of hair, paused to return Fargo's glance.

"He giving you trouble, Miss Donna?" the sergeant asked in a growling, deep voice.

"No, it's all right, Jamison," Donna said, and the soldier, his heavy face truculent, led the horse away. "Sergeant Jamison is Daddy's aide. He's protective about me," she explained.

"Maybe you ought to take him with you next time you go riding."

"Dammit, Fargo, I went with you because I wanted to go with you," she said, a half-pout touching her lips.

"Maybe I'll give you another chance," he said, and wheeled the pinto away. He rode into town and reined up at the saloon, where the bartender nodded to him.

"You find Pecosito?" the man asked, and Fargo nodded.

"Now I'd like to find something to eat with my tequila," he said.

"You are in the right place. We serve food here," the barkeep said. "Texas beef, mule deer, peccary."

"Texas beef," Fargo said, and took his drink to a table. His eyes dismissed two of the girls who strolled up. He let the tequila relax his spirit and body. The beef came atop black bread, but it was tasty enough and he ate quickly and strolled from the saloon, pausing only to see it was quickly growing crowded with too many drifters for his tastes, a few even bringing their own girls.

He took the Ovaro and rode up the hillsides until he reached the big bur oak and bedded down for the night. But Pecosito's words kept buzzing through his thoughts as though they were a swarm of annoying gnats. And with them, Major Danton Honegger kept intruding into his thoughts.

The man had invited a United States senator and a party of journalists to watch him control and subdue the Mescalero when he had no control of them at all. It made no damn sense. He was putting himself on display where it seemed he could only fail abysmally. Conceit could make men fools, Fargo knew. He'd seen that before. Was he witnessing that again? Was Danton Honegger so conceited that he actually thought he could demonstrate his control over the Mescalero? Or was there more? If so, what in hell could it be? Honegger had admitted he was a man of ambition who despised this assignment. But General Redfield had said he'd proven himself a fool and an incompetent once. Maybe this was only more of the same. It was the easiest explanation, and yet it failed to satisfy. Danton Honegger seemed far too calculating to be that kind of fool. Or was he? Fargo swore softly. The thought continued to revolve without an answer and he forced his mind to shake away further speculation. He closed his eyes and drew sleep around himself and hoped the new day might bring new thoughts.

3

The sun rose quickly after Fargo woke, shimmering across the land. When he'd washed and dressed, he breakfasted on a stand of Indian figs, their tart-sweet taste worth all the effort of getting at the inner pulp. Sometime during the night, his subconscious mind had made a decision. He would pay Pecosito another visit, alone this time. Perhaps there was more the trader would tell him that way. Besides, he wanted Pecosito to take him to where he could follow the soldier and the Mescalero. Maybe he would find something. Searching, seeking, reading signs—that was the way of his life, to see where other men only looked.

Fargo turned the Ovaro out from beside the prickly pear and slowly began to ride across the sculptured land, moving in a wide circle as he neared the sandstone formations. He searched the flat ledges where the troopers had been positioned, half-expecting to find them there again, but they were gone. He rode on to the next red-clay rocks and found they were silent and empty, also. His grim smile held satisfaction. The major was not entirely a fool. Or he had decided not to risk losing any more of his troopers. Fargo turned the Ovaro around and headed south toward Red Bluff Lake.

The sun was moving through the afternoon sky when he reached the oblong body of crystal-clear water. He circled the shore and came to the wickiup, slowly rode to a halt, and dismounted. He paused, waiting for the small figure to appear in the doorway, but the opening remained empty.

"Pecosito," he called, and received no answer. Tiny hairs on the back of his neck suddenly stiffened and his hand went to the big Colt at his hip. He moved to one side and came up on the doorway of the hut with the gun in his hand. He halted, listened, and heard only silence. He swung his body sharply, dropped into a half-crouch, the six-gun ready to fire, and scanned the interior of the wickiup with a sweeping glance. The hut was empty and he heard the rush of breath leave him as he straightened up and holstered the gun. He turned and went back outside, strolled around to the rear of the wickiup to see the small brown horse tethered to a long rope. It was Pecosito's horse, the same one he'd had for years, Fargo knew. He turned to peer into the brush and trees behind the hut.

Pecosito could have gone for a short walk, he told himself, trying unsuccessfully to ignore the apprehension that continued to stab at him. But he couldn't. Instead, he turned and marched into the hut. He halted inside the wickiup and frowned at the wooden chair broken in one corner, pieces of firewood scattered across the floor, and his eyes went to the wicker mats used for sitting. One had been pushed almost to the wall, another bunched together, and the third lay at a crazy angle. He dropped to one knee. They had been used for more than relaxation, and he spotted the six-gun on the floor of the hut where it had skittered to rest against one wall. His eyes grew hard as he saw the stains on the mat.

He bent closer and saw the stains were the dark red of blood, not much more than ten or twelve hours old, and the curse stuck in his throat as he straightened up and was outside in two long strides. He peered at the ground at the other side of the hut and saw a pair of marks across the soil, tracks where someone had been dragged away. Pecosito had been that someone, he was certain. He followed the marks to where they ended at hoofprints led into the hawthorn and he followed on foot as he spotted the small drops of blood that made a clear trail.

The trail came to an abrupt end as he found the crumpled form lying in the woods. He bent down, pressed his face to the little man's mouth as he hoped to catch even the faintest gasped breath. But there was nothing. Pecosito was dead.

Fargo turned the small form on its back. He'd not been shot, Fargo saw. The man's head was furrowed with deep, red gashes. "Damn," Fargo swore. He lifted the cold form and carried it back to the wickiup. He had just reached the end of the hawthorn when he halted, slid Pecosito to the ground, and reached down to pick up the yellow object that had caught his eye. It was a button, a very distinctive button, the kind that came from the uniform of a United States cavalryman. He slipped the button into his pocket. His face had grown hard as a stone.

Fargo found a shovel inside the hut and used it to dig a shallow grave nearby. He had no idea what his friend's spiritual beliefs were, or if he had any at all, so he put a small wooden cross inside a triangle of stones and a garland of hawthorn leaves atop it. He paused again inside the wickiup and surveyed the jars of coins and the beads and baubles. Those who came to visit would take what they wanted. Within the month there'd be nothing left but the bare walls of branches and twigs. He climbed onto his horse as the day began to close to an end. He rode slowly away, his mouth a tight, grim line.

The Trailsman rode through the darkness, and it was near midnight when he drew near to the tall shape of the stockade wall. He saw the front gate half-closed, the two sentries on watch, and he stayed in the deep shadows out of their sight as he circled to the rear of the stockade before moving closer. As he had expected, there were two rear doors. He paused at each and found they were latched from inside. He slid from the Ovaro and took his lariat, fashioned a small loop at one end, and stepped back. With a long, arching motion he tossed the lariat into the air and watched it hit the top of the stockade wall. He pulled gently and the loop caught itself around one of the pointed ends of the stockade wall. He pulled again, made sure the loop was securely caught, and then began to pull himself up the side of the stockade wall. He halted when he reached the top, his gaze scanning the other side. The only sentries were the two at the top of the wall by the front gate, and Fargo climbed over the stockade and dropped to one knee on the catwalk that ran along the inner edge of the wall.

He pulled the lariat up after him and used it again to lower himself to the ground inside the silent, sleeping fort. He yanked the lariat down and tied it around his waist. He moved in a half-crouch across the darkness of the square and came to a halt at the low-roofed structure that was the major's quarters. He crept forward, past one window, and listened to the sound of a man's half-snoring breaths, moved on to the next window, and stopped again. The bottom half of the window was almost all the way open and he caught the faint scent of powder and perfume. Extending one long leg over the sill and twisting his back low, he climbed into the the room and saw the bed near the other window. Even in the almost total darkness he could see the dry-wheat shock of hair against the pillow and he stepped forward to halt at the bed. She half-sensed something and turned, and he saw the long line of one breast almost fall from the neck of the pink nightgown.

He pressed his hand down over her mouth and Donna Honegger's eyes snapped open at once, fright seizing the light-gray spheres. She blinked, focused, and stared at him, a frown of recognition sliding across her face.

"We're going someplace where we can talk," Fargo muttered harshly. "You make one sound and somebody gets hurt, maybe even dead. You understand."

She nodded. He drew his hand from her mouth and pulled her to her feet, taking in the way the pink nightgown lay against her belly and clung to the long curve of her thighs.

"Turn around while I put some clothes on," Donna said.

"No. You'll go that way. It's a hot night," Fargo whispered back. She started to protest again but he cut her off. "Take your clothes. You can change later," he said, and waited while she gathered a riding skirt and a blouse before he took her arm and steered her to the window. He crawled outside, one hand holding on to her wrist, and pulled her out after him. He paused, his eyes moving across the grounds

53

of the fort, rising to the two sentries at the top of the front gate. The fort remained hard asleep and he hurried her to the back of the stockade and halted at one of the two doors. He unlatched it and stepped outside with Donna, aware that she stared at him with a mixture of bewilderment and apprehension. He climbed onto the Ovaro, pulled her up to sit in front of him, and felt the warm softness of her against him. He walked the horse until he was far enough away to go in a slow canter.

"Can we talk now?" Donna asked.

"No," he snapped, and kept the pinto moving forward at a steady pace. He slowed only when he reached the big bur oak, where he reined to a stop. "Off," he barked, and Donna slipped from the pinto, stepping a dozen feet away as Fargo swung from the horse to face her, his chiseled handsomeness hard and tight with anger. She held the clothes she'd taken against her breasts.

"May I dress, first?" she said coldly, and he turned his back on her, listening to the sounds of her pulling on shirt and skirt. When she finished, he turned and saw she held the pink nightgown in her hands, her light-gray eyes regarding him with a mixture of curiosity and irritation. "Now would you tell me what this is all about," she snapped.

"You've a big mouth," Fargo growled. "I'd never have taken you along if I thought you were going to run to Daddy and tell him where you'd been and what you heard."

Surprise flashed in her eyes but only for an instant as she recovered quickly. "I didn't," she said.

Fargo's hand snapped out, curled around the front of her shirt, and he yanked her forward. "Don't lie to me, dammit," he bit out. "You told him, and Pecosito's dead."

Donna Honegger's mouth fell open and he saw the shock and horror cloud the light-gray eyes. He took his hand from her and she continued to stare at him. "No, oh, no," she breathed.

"Yes, damn you."

She swallowed, brought her lips together, and shook away the initial shock. "My father had nothing to do with it," she murmured. "He wouldn't do something like that."

"But you did tell him, didn't you? Why, goddammit?" Fargo barked.

She closed her eyes for a moment, and when she pulled them open, he saw the pain inside the light-gray orbs. "It was his price," she murmured. "He was going to court-martial the three troopers and arrest you."

"Arrest me? What in hell for?"

"For urging a soldier to leave his post. It's part of some obscure army regulation. He said he'd the right to invoke it," Donna said. "But he told me he'd do nothing if I found out what you were up to, and I agreed. I thought it was the right thing to do, for the troopers and for you."

Fargo searched her face and saw only shock and pain in it and she half-turned, sank down atop a small hillock.

"My God, that nice little man . . . dead. How terrible," she murmured, and moments later she lifted her eyes to the big man standing over her. "Anybody could've killed him. You've no right to just go off assuming my father did it. That's not fair."

"I don't go around assuming," Fargo said, and

drew the button from his pocket. He held it out in his palm and watched as she stared at it. "I found this near Pecosito's place," he said.

Donna stared at the button and finally wrenched her eyes from it with an effort. He slipped it back into his pocket. "He didn't do it, never. He wouldn't," she murmured.

"He gives orders," Fargo remarked.

She rose and flung words at him through pain, her voice breaking. "You found a button. Maybe it doesn't mean anything. I don't know."

"I know you went back and shot your mouth off, and the next morning Pecosito is dead. I say that means something, especially after what he told us," Fargo said.

"I don't know what it means. Maybe it was all a coincidence," Donna insisted. "I didn't bring it about. It wasn't my fault. Oh, God, no, please don't say that." She fell against his chest, sobs bursting from her, her arms around his neck as she clung tight against him. He felt the soft points of her breasts press his body.

He put his arms around her and held her, letting her sobs subside. He wouldn't press further for now, not till he was more certain. "All right, ease off, honey," he said gently, and stroked the dry-wheat hair. "You did wrong, but you were trying to do right. That makes a difference."

"Thank you," she said, her face grave as she looked up at him, a plea for understanding in the light-gray eyes.

"I'll take you back," he said.

"No," she blurted, her hand catching at his arm. "I don't want to go back, not now. I don't want to be there. I don't know why. I just don't."

56

"It's called not knowing what to believe and what to feel," Fargo said quietly.

"That collision course with myself?" Donna said, and he nodded. "I'll go back in the morning," she said, asking in her voice.

"Suit yourself," he said, and started to take his bedroll down. "I'm going to get some shut-eye." He set the bedroll out and quickly began to undress. He halted when he was down to his underdrawers, then he stretched out on the bedroll. She folded herself down to sit beside him, her eyes moving across the beautifully muscled symmetry of his body. He let her eyes enjoy what they saw and watched her tongue come out to moisten the dryness of her lips.

"Go on, say it," Fargo remarked softly.

"I was thinking about the first time I saw this body, when you were a Mescalero," Donna said.

"That's not all you're thinking." He smiled and she let her thin eyebrows arch. "You're thinking you'd like me to make love to you."

She had an instant frown. "I'm not thinking any such thing."

He sat up on one elbow and brushed his hand across the yellow hair. "The hell you're not," he said softly.

"No, you're wrong," she said, but he heard the sudden nervousness in her voice. "You couldn't. I mean, I wouldn't respond."

He laughed. A challenge wrapped in denial. "You're sure about that, Donna?" He continued to run his hand through her hair.

She lifted her head and met his eyes with a direct stare. "Yes, of course I'm sure," she answered, the nervousness still in her voice.

He let his hand stop at the back of her neck and

gently rubbed his thumb back and forth across the little stray wisps of yellow hair. Firmly but gently, he drew her face toward him, his hand still rubbing the back of her neck. He met the light-gray eyes, saw the indecision swimming in their depths, and closed his lips over hers. He pressed gently, felt the softness of her mouth even as she held back.

He paused and her voice was a whisper. "You see?" she said, and his answer was to press his mouth onto hers again, still ever so gently, adding a touch more demand, then letting his tongue dart out to flicker against her lips for an instant. "You see?" she said again. But this time the words were hardly audible and he suddenly pressed hard against her lips. He heard her short gasped moment of breath and felt her lips open, grow wet and soft. "Oh," she murmured. "Oh." His mouth covered hers and his tongue thrust forward. Donna's mouth opened, met the sweet hunger of his, and he felt her hands flatten against his chest, her fingers digging into his skin as her lips answered, worked with his now, drawing his mouth into her own.

"You see?" Fargo murmured.

Donna let a long sigh escape her as her hands moved down across the smoothly muscled contours of his chest, down to his abdomen, held there and pressed into him. He undid the buttons of her skirt with quick, deft motions and she wriggled out of the garment and slid onto the bedroll, her longish breasts turned nicely at the bottoms with very large dark-pink areolae surrounding tall, already firm points of a slightly darker shade. He pulled at the buttons at the side of the skirt and they came open at once, his hand pushing the garment from her. Donna drew her legs up together, turned herself into him but covered herself, trembled, and held there in a moment of modesty and sudden reluctance. He drew his mouth from hers, lowered his lips onto one longish breast, and drew the firm, pink tip into his mouth, pulled gently, and heard Donna's shuddered cry. He drew the soft breast deeper into his mouth and her voice rose, and when his hand pressed into her drawn-up thighs, she half-turned, cried out again as her lips lowered and fell open.

"Oh, God," Donna breathed as he paused and took in a long figure, flat belly, and wide hips, everything with just enough flesh on it to add softness to angularness, a bushy, almost blond nap pointing the way to thighs that carried enough flesh to add a long curve to their length. She turned to him and in her eyes he saw something close to wonder, almost a kind of self-protest even as she reached up and drew his face down to her breasts.

"Aaaah . . . aaaah," Donna murmured as he took their soft-firm points into his mouth and caressed each, pulled, and sucked. He heard her cry out in delight.

"You see?" he murmured against her breasts, and felt her nod.

"Yes, damn you, yes," Donna Honegger breathed. She pushed her breasts upward with sudden fierceness. "More, more, oh, God, more."

He pulled on the warm soft cups, let one hand move down along her flat belly and come to rest on the bushy, blond nap, and he felt her hips lift at once. "Oh . . . ooooh," Donna gasped. Her hand suddenly came to clasp on top of his, pressing his fingers deeper into her until he was holding hard against the small mount of Venus under the wiry softness.

"Uuuuh . . . uuuh . . . uuuh," Donna began to moan, the sound growing in intensity as his fingers moved, dropped lower, and pressed down into the warmth of her still-clasped thighs. Her legs moved apart at once, and when he cupped the wet warmth of her, she screamed into the warm night. Her voice suddenly dropped an octave, became almost a growl. "Take me, Fargo . . . my God, please, please." She twisted her torso, begging with her opened thighs. He swung atop her and pressed his tumescent, flaming organ into her pubic mound. "Aaaaah, ah, ah, God," Donna breathed at the touch, and her voice rose in a wild cry of desire as he moved, brought his godhead down to her wet, flowing entrance. She screamed, held there as she half-cried, half-sobbed with wanting.

He moved slowly into her smooth pathway of eager flesh, full of the touch of consummate pleasure. He felt her legs move to encircle him as she put her head back, the dry-wheat hair falling in yellow profusion. He moved with delicious sensations surrounding him and heard his own groans match her gasped cries. Donna moved with him, crying out in rhythm to split the hot night with shuddered screams. He put his mouth down on the longish breasts as the wondrous moment went on seemingly without end. Donna Honegger clasped arms and legs around him in a sudden, desperate seizure, and he heard her cries spiral into a long, shrieking wail. "Now, now, now . . . Oh, God, iiiiiiaaaaa . . . Now, nooooowww . . ." She wailed and shuddered. He felt her clinging around him as he exploded with her, sharing the ecstasy of the timeless moment until he fell limply beside her. She lay trembling, drawing in deep breaths. She reached for his hand, found it, and pressed it on top of one long breast, curled his fingers around the soft cup, and uttered a tiny groan of satisfaction.

Seconds that seemed minutes, minutes that seemed hours, the aftermath of passion, sweet satiation, and she turned against him finally, clung to him, and lay silent, sleep drawing itself over her. She stirred finally, brought her eyes open, and stared at him. "How did you know?" she whispered.

"There was wanting, needing, and running. Put them all together and they spelled only one thing," Fargo told her.

"It doesn't change what I believe."

"Didn't expect so," Fargo said. "You going to carry tales again when you go back?"

"No," Donna said. "You'll be doing that, I expect."

"I will," he agreed grimly, and she pushed up on one elbow, reached out for her skirt. He watched her draw clothes on and enjoyed the way her breasts swung gently. He rose and dressed when she'd finished, and when they began the ride back, she picked up on the question that came into his mind.

"We'll go through the front gate," she said.

"There'll be talk," he said. "Daddy might be up. It'll be about dawn when we get there."

"I don't care," she said, defiance curled around each word.

He held her to him as they rode, a gesture that offered only outer comfort to inner wounds. He rode unhurriedly and the dawn sky had just begun to streak the sky when he rode into the fort with Donna. He saw the two sentries look on with surprise as he let her down from the pinto outside the major's quarters and slowly rode away. He returned almost to the big bur oak but found a smaller tree that sufficed for him to get in a few hours of sound sleep, and when he woke again, the sun warmed his body.

4

When Fargo reached the fort once again, the sun was in the midmorning sky. Honegger watched from the doorway as the Trailsman rode to a halt. The major's normally disdainful expression was joined by one of pompous anger. "I must say you have your nerve coming in here now," the man said. "Brass and bad taste, that's what it is."

"Almost as bad taste as murder and bushwhacking," Fargo said, and the major's eyes narrowed.

"What's that supposed to mean?" Danton Honegger's stare waited, but Fargo swung from his horse and strolled to the doorway.

"I think you'll like it better if we talk inside," Fargo said. The major hesitated a moment, then led the way into his office. "Donna told you part of it," Fargo said.

"Yes, about my sneaking off to meet with the Mescalero in the dead of night. Preposterous," Honegger sneered.

"So preposterous that my contact was killed the day after you heard about it."

Honegger's thin face darkened. "You watch what you're saying, Fargo," he shot back. "He was an old recluse and backwoods trader. Anybody could've killed him, including the Mescalero."

Fargo tossed the button on the desk and let the man stare at it. "Found it where he was killed," he said.

"Doesn't mean a damn thing. There are a hundred ways it could've gotten there. He might have a dozen more lying around someplace for trading. And as for his story about seeing a soldier ride off with the Mescalero, that's all shit," the major said. "I'll tell you what he saw. He saw another Mescalero wearing an army jacket and pants taken from some slain soldier. You know they scavenge clothing every time they can, especially uniforms. It was night. He admitted that. He saw what I just told you, that's all. Now I don't intend to hear any more about it. The man made a mistake."

"Three times?" Fargo put in evenly.

"Yes, dammit, three times," Honegger roared. "Now get the hell out of my office and stay away from my daughter."

"She's a big girl. She can do whatever she wants to do. So can I, and don't you forget that, mister," Fargo said, his voice growing hard. He left the major with the man's lips quivering in anger, strode outside, and saw Donna emerge from a side door.

"I heard from the other room," she said. "What he said makes sense, Fargo. You have to admit that. It was night. Pecosito could have made a mistake, even three times."

Fargo allowed a tolerant smile. "You might make a mistake. Anybody might. Even me. But not Pecosito. He'd know a Mescalero when he saw one no matter what he was wearing, especially three times. And it's damn funny he's suddenly killed right after Daddy heard about what he'd seen. He'd lived a life-

64

time there, and all of a sudden somebody comes and kills him.''

Donna looked unhappy as she answered. ''Things sometimes happen that way. There are coincidences,'' she tried.

''There's also steer shit,'' Fargo snapped.

''But it doesn't add up, doesn't make sense. You said that yourself,'' Donna reminded him.

''That's the one thing right. It doesn't make any damn sense for the Mescalero to be talking to him,'' Fargo said. ''So I'm going to keep nosing around until I find something that does make sense.''

She started to turn away, the unhappiness still in her face, and she paused. ''I want to see you again,'' she said. ''Maybe that doesn't make any sense either, but I want to.''

He tossed her a grin. ''That makes its own sense.''

''When?'' Donna asked as he pulled himself into the saddle.

''I'll let you know,'' he said, and started from the fort. He rode north, turned, and moved across the dry land in a wide circle south, slowly veering west. He turned up into a line of red clay and sandstone hills. There he halted on an open ledge and let the Ovaro rest. Fargo's eyes were cold as a midwinter lake, his chiseled face tight. He was being followed. He had picked up the faint spiral of dust soon after he'd left the fort; he had taken the circuitous route on purpose to see if the rider stayed with him.

Fargo remained in the open and knew his pursuer was drawing closer. He gave the rider another few minutes and then moved the Ovaro forward from the ledge and higher into the jagged mountain country.

He turned into a narrow passageway, made no effort to be quiet as the pinto's hooves echoed on the stone underfoot. His eyes scanning the twisting, jagged shapes of the almost treeless terrain, he spotted a small stone clearing, rode the Ovaro into it, and dismounted. He led the horse to the far end, left him there, and scrambled on foot up to a narrow ledge overlooking the clearing. Crouched, he watched the passage with the silent patience of a horned lizard waiting for its prey to come within range. The wait was longer than he'd expected, and he was just beginning to conclude that his pursuer had lost the trail when the shot rang out. He felt the bullet graze the top of his ear and he threw himself forward as a second shot rang out from above him, this one sending a spray of stone chips into his face. There was no place to even twist or turn on the narrow ledge, much less hide, and he cursed silently. He had underestimated his pursuer. Every muscle tensed, he let himself go over the edge of the ledge, pressed his shoulder against the stone to slow the fall.

He twisted his body to land on both shoulders and his back, but felt the pain shoot through his body as he came down on the stone ledge. He half-turned limply and lay still. From above the ledge, it would seem that one of the shots had hit its mark. He remained motionless, eyes all but closed. After a moment passed he heard the sound of a horse moving slowly down one of the passages from above the clearing and he swore at himself again. The horse came down into the clearing and he heard the rider dismount, walk toward him, and through slitted eyes he saw the stiff leather of army riding boots. The tip of the barrel of an army Winchester came into view, but the holder had the rifle pointed to the side with misplaced confidence. Fargo gathered every muscle in his powerful body, paused an extra split second, and exploded. He wrapped one arm around the legs in front of him as he kicked out at the same time. The figure fell forward and Fargo felt his foot connect with a head. He heard a curse of pain as he leapt up and saw the figure roll, the rifle skitter across the stone, and a heavy face with short-cropped hair came into his sight.

"Sergeant Jamison," Fargo breathed, and saw the man rush at him, a bull-like charge. He started to reach for his Colt but halted. He wanted Jamison alive, able to answer questions. The man barreled forward and Fargo stepped sideways, bringing down a chopping blow that caught the charging figure along the side of the head. The sergeant stumbled and fell on his hands and knees. Fargo rushed to bring another blow down, but the man kicked out backwards, as a mule kicks, and Fargo felt the explosion of pain as the blow caught him full in the groin. He went down, his lips drawn back, rolled, and avoided Jamison's next kick as the man rose and spun. Groaning in pain, Fargo let himself roll again as the man leapt onto him and he felt fingers clutching at his throat. Ignoring the pain that shot through his body, Fargo managed to bring up a short blow that sank into Jamison's midsection. Though it had only traveled inches from a poor angle, it was enough to make the sergeant grunt, lose a rush of breath, and pull his fingers back from Fargo's throat.

Fargo brought one knee up and pushed. The sergeant went sideways and rolled onto his back. Fighting off the waves of pain that still shot through him, Fargo went after the soldier, but Jamison scuttled backward, rolled, and leapt to his feet. He came in with a swinging left and a follow-up right, and Fargo ducked both, trying for a short uppercut that missed as Jamison managed to pull away.

Cursing, Jamison came in again. Fargo blocked both wild punches, ducked low, let Jamison get off two more blows, and smashed a short left hook upward. It caught Jamison on the jaw and the man flew backward and went down. He shook his head and saw Fargo coming, rolled, and made a dive for where the Winchester lay. Fargo leapt forward as he saw Jamison's hand almost at the rifle and brought his foot down on the man's fingers.

Jamison screamed in pain, yanked his hand back, and Fargo came at him. The sergeant rose to a crouch, turned, and started to race toward the passageway.

"Hold it right there," Fargo yelled, but Jamison only glanced back and kept running. Fargo yanked the Colt from its holster and pulled the hammer back. "Stop, dammit," he ordered, but Jamison was at the entranceway to the passage.

Fargo aimed low and fired and saw the bullet smash into the sergeant's leg. Jamison half-screamed in pain, dropped to one knee, but pulled himself up and half-ran, half-dragged himself into the passage. "Damn," Fargo swore as the man disappeared into the passage. His groin still afire, he nonetheless broke into a run and chased after Jamison. He heard the clatter of loose stone and saw the man climbing up on the pinnacled rocks.

The sergeant left a blood-streaked trail from his leg as he climbed, but out of fear or desperation, he kept climbing. With a silent oath, Fargo started up the rocks after him, holstered the Colt again so he could climb, and saw Jamison making surprising speed up along the high, sharp-spired formation.

"Damn," Fargo swore, and began to pull himself up along the rocks. Jamison had found a series of steplike indentations along the high spire of weather-hardened sandstone and was proceeding quickly in spite of his leg. Fargo kept his eyes on the man as he pulled up on the rock and glanced away for only a brief instant to secure a better hold for himself when he heard Jamison's voice, a half-curse first, then a scream.

The Trailsman looked up to see the sergeant starting to fall backward through the air as a piece of rock he had grabbed hold of came loose. Jamison might have been able to recover his balance had he two good legs, but the bullet-shattered one only helped to send him toppling. Fargo winced as he saw the man bounce off the side of one spire, hit against another sharp point, and hurtle down between two jagged slabs of stone. Jamison's wailing scream came to a sharp, sudden end.

Fargo swore as he changed directions and carefully began to work his way down and across to where the man had fallen. He found the sergeant finally, at the bottom of a crevice, a broken, still form, and he made his way carefully down the steep sides, lowering himself on the narrow protrusions of stone.

When he reached the bottom, he stared down at the man. He had hoped to find some life still in the shattered body but there was none. However, as he stared at the sergeant, he saw the two brass buttons on the left sleeve of the man's uniform. The third, top button was missing.

Fargo knelt, fished the button from his pocket,

and placed it against the sleeve of the uniform where it plainly belonged. A grim snort escaped him as he pushed to his feet and dropped the button into his pocket. He had one answer: Jamison had killed Pecosito. But that's all he had. The real answer still danced tantalizingly out of reach. Had Jamison acted on his own or on order?

Fargo knew damn well what he believed, but knowing was one thing and proving another. Jamison was the major's aide, but that still was no hard proof. The man could have had something going for himself on the side. Honegger would claim exactly that, of course, Fargo knew, and he swore as he began to climb back to where he'd left the Ovaro.

When he reached the horse he retraced steps down from the jagged spires of stone. It still made no damn sense that the major would be dealing with the Mescalero. Or they with him. Yet Pecosito was dead for what he had seen. Fargo grimaced and felt not unlike a fire fighter who could find only the smoke and not the fire. But the flame had to be there someplace. He only hoped he could find it before it blazed out of control.

He reached the flat land, put the Ovaro into a trot, and headed back to town. The afternoon was winding down when he neared the fort and saw a squad of troopers in close-order drill outside the stockade. They rode smartly, he noted, and executed their turns with precision. A young lieutenant barked commands as he looked on, and Fargo paused beside him. "They won't be on parade when they face off with the Mescalero," Fargo said.

"Meaning what, sir?" the lieutenant asked.

"They'll need stamina and crafty riding, not precision," Fargo said, and moved on into the fort.

Inside the stockade he saw the major putting a smaller squad on foot through an honor-guard drill. Donna, in a dark-green dress, looked on. The major dismissed the squad when the Ovaro came to a halt. "Expecting your distinguished visitors soon?" Fargo asked.

"Tomorrow," the major answered.

"You looking for Sergeant Jamison?" Fargo inquired casually.

"He had some free time coming. He went off on his own," the major said.

"Don't expect him back," Fargo said. Danton Honegger's faintly disdainful countenance showed no change in expression, Fargo noted. But he saw Donna's thin brows arch.

"Why not?" the major asked.

"He tried some climbing on the high rocks. He failed the course," Fargo said, and this time Honegger's eyes narrowed.

"He have any help in failing?" the man slid out.

"He might have." Fargo shrugged. "Can't say for sure. But he's the one who killed Pecosito. That's for sure. That button matched the missing one on his sleeve."

"Apparently my sergeant was into something on his own," the major said.

Fargo smiled. "Sort of figured you'd say that." He saw the major's face harden.

"You watch yourself, Fargo, especially when the senator arrives. I don't care if General Redfield sent you down here. Any more sideways accusations and I'll chase your tail out of here," the man said.

Fargo's eyes hardened and he caught the dismay in Donna's face as she listened. "All right, no more sideways accusations. Either you're a goddamn fool and you're going to get all your men killed trying to put on a show for the senator, or you're up to something else. I'm going to find out which before it's too late, if I can. Is that plain enough for you?'' he said.

"Quite,'' Honegger said, and cold anger replaced his normal disdain. He spun on his heel and stalked into the building.

Fargo turned his eyes to Donna.

"That was uncalled for,'' she said, and he saw that her protectiveness had reasserted itself. "I think you just can't believe that Daddy can subdue the Mescalero.''

"You're damn right there,'' Fargo said.

"Why is that so impossible for you to believe?''

"Because he doesn't know the first thing about fighting the Mescalero. Hell, he proved that much by setting his men out to be picked off. From what I hear, he doesn't know how to fight any Indians, and the Mescalero take a special knowledge.''

"Why?''

"Because they're trickier than most, more savage than most, and smarter than most. They can be handled, but by someone with real field experience, someone who knows how, not by somebody who wants to impress a senator,'' Fargo said.

"If he fails, it'll be his loss, his command that will suffer, his reputation that will go down. It seems to me that's none of your concern, or of General Redfield,'' Donna said stiffly.

"It's not that simple, honey,'' Fargo answered. "Even if you forget all the good young men he'll sacrifice on the altar of stupidity, this post is the only protection the ranchers and towns have around here. Maybe it's not a hell of a lot under Daddy, but it is something. He lets the command be wiped out, the

72

Mescalero will go on a rampage and it'll take months before the army sends in replacements. A lot of people will be dead by then.''

Donna took his words in but he saw she remained stiff and protective. ''I say none of that's going to happen. He'll prove you wrong. What will you say when he does?'' she asked.

''Amen and hallelujah,'' Fargo said. ''Seeing this is plain-talk time, you still want to wrestle in the hay tonight?''

She swallowed, hesitated, but protectiveness and loyalty were in the driver's seat. ''I don't think the mood is right. All this accusing upsets me. I'm sorry.''

Fargo laughed. ''You'll be more sorry later, about midnight.'' He wheeled the pinto around and rode away. Dusk had begun to blanket the land. He rode hard, turned south but not to Red Bluff Lake. Instead, he edged westward and rode under the almost full moon that rose into the dark, velvet sky.

The moon had touched the midnight sky when he slowed at the foothills of the Guadalupe Mountains, rockbound with a good cover of hackberry, smooth sumac, and juniper. He moved the pinto through the foothills, following the natural contours of the land. He drew in deep drafts of air, his nostrils flaring every few moments. Suddenly he halted and slid from the pinto. He pulled the horse into a deep thicket and left it tethered to a low branch before hurrying forward on foot. He could smell the Mescalero camp wood fires burning low, the odor of hides readied for drying and cutting, and most of all, the permeating scent of bodies covered with fish oil and vegetable dye.

The Trailsman picked his way closer until the

camp came into sight, silent and sleeping. That was why he had come now, to find a spot for himself to watch when the morning dawned. He knew he'd never be able to get close enough if he tried by day. He moved forward again, as near as he dared, and chose a tall hackberry. Carefully he climbed into the thick foliages of its branches. He found a spot that formed a kind of cradle to support his torso and let him lean his head back and he settled in, closed his eyes, and drew sleep around himself.

The position wasn't as uncomfortable as it would seem. He slept well and woke with the first gray light of dawn. He could see the entire camp. A line of wickiups stretched along one side, and at the far end was a collection of tepees. The squaws were up first, he saw, tending the fires that smoldered and preparing a form of millet biscuit.

Fargo, silent as a chicken hawk looking down at a barnyard, watched the braves wake and finally, from the largest wickiup, the figure strolled into the open. He wore only cut-down white man's trousers, revealing well-muscled shoulders. A brow band held his long, thick black hair back from the side of his face. Coronado, Fargo murmured to himself as he saw the others treat the man with respect, falling to the sides when he strode by. The Mescalero chief had narrow eyes that let only a small portion of his black pupils shine forth. A strong, hawk-nosed face held cruelty in it, the thin mouth turning down at the corners.

One of the squaws brought the chief a millet cake and another a pouch of water. After he'd eaten and drunk, Coronado faced the others who gathered around and spoke to them in a dialect of the Athapaskan tongue most of the Apache used. Fargo knew only enough of the language to catch a few words here and there. When the chief broke into a few phrases of Spanish every once in a while, he understood a little more. But one thing came across with utmost clarity: Mangas Coronado was a man who not only exuded confidence but also seemed very pleased with himself.

When he finished his address and turned away, his warriors gave out with a cheerlike chant. Another Mescalero, a tall, thin man with an army knife stuck in his waistband, halted beside the chief and Coronado pointed to the south, spoke in low tones, and then laughed with a harsh sound. He returned inside his wickiup and Fargo watched the others tend to their chores, some forming arrows, a few cleaning rifles, most tending to their bows.

The sun had begun to move toward the noon sky when Coronado emerged again, strode to where a line of barebacked ponies were tethered, and led some twenty of his warriors into the woods to the south.

All in all, Fargo had counted a little over a hundred Mescalero warriors in the camp, but the tepees and wickiups could hold not more than sixty to seventy, he estimated. That meant there were at least some thirty new arrivals. He tucked the fact into a corner of his mind and began to carefully and silently climb from the tree. He'd seen what he wanted to see, and he knew where the camp was now. He'd not have to waste precious time searching if he wanted to come again. And he had seen Mangas Coronado, a true Mescalero chief made of confidence and cruelty. He winced as he thought of Danton Honegger going into battle against this man.

Fargo reached the ground and immediately dropped to his stomach. He began to crawl, inching his back back through the trees so there wouldn't be the slightest sound, not the risk of a snapped twig or a branch brushed back too hard. He was nearing the Ovaro when he heard the sound of horses moving through the tree to his left. He glimpsed a half-dozen Mescalero heading toward the camp, not those Coronado had taken with him. These came from the east, he saw. More new arrivals, he took note. He waited until they disappeared and went on to the Ovaro. He didn't get to his feet till he was deep in the thicket beside the horse, and then, the Colt in his hand, he began to lead the pinto out of the dense foliage.

He didn't swing onto the horse till he'd reached the bottom of the foothills. When he did, he turned east, back the way he'd come, finally swinging northward toward Dry Lake. He let idle thoughts flow through his mind as he rode at a steady, unhurried pace. There was more than the major's stupidity and incompetence that bothered him. That was too easy an explanation, and it didn't account for whatever Pecosito had seen and been killed for seeing. There was something more, and somehow, someway, it revolved around Danton Honegger. But perhaps not around his stupidity, Fargo pondered. Perhaps it revolved around his ambitions, the demonstration he wanted to put on for the senator and the journalists. But could the one be separated from the other? Weren't they peas in the same pod? It seemed so, and yet something told him there was more.

Fargo pushed the spinning questions from his

mind as he came in sight of the fort. They'd not go far, he was certain, and he hurried forward to where he saw the line of troopers at attention outside the gate.

5

He glimpsed the stagecoach with an escort of six troopers approach the fort as he reached the gate and drew to one side. Major Honegger walked from the stockade, Donna beside him in a pink dress that, with the dry-wheat hair, made her look fragile and delicate and very lovely. She saw him and tossed him an almost sheepish smile. Major Honegger wore his very best authoritative manner, Fargo noted. It was plain that he'd had patrols out looking for the stagecoach, and when they reported sighting it, he'd brought the post out for a proper reception.

The stagecoach, dust-covered, with the canvas down on the windows, rolled to a halt. Fargo dismounted, edging closer as the major and Donna approached the wagon. The stage door opened and a man clambered down, on the portly side, a frock coat and a four-in-hand giving him an out-of-place formality. Fargo took in a round, bland face that was not matched by a pair of very sharp, piercing eyes.

"Senator Thurston, welcome to Fort Midland," the major said, and the senator clasped his outstretched hand. "Donna, my daughter. Senator Roy Thurston," Honegger introduced.

"My pleasure, ma'am," the senator said in a strong, almost booming voice. "Didn't expect the trip to be so goddamn hot, I don't mind telling you, major," the man said.

"We have something nice and cool for you to drink inside, Senator," the major said, and suddenly turned back to the stage as a young woman emerged. "But I'm neglecting the rest of your party," he said.

"Ellie Rogers," the young woman said. "You go along with the senator. I want to see to my bags first. I'll join you."

"Please do," Honegger said, and went with the senator as the man gave his honor guard a cursory inspection and hurried into the building with Donna and her father.

Fargo strolled to the stage, where the driver handed two traveling bags to the young woman. "Excuse me, but where are the journalists?" he asked. "They come by another stage?"

"You're looking at them," she said, and Fargo realized he was too late to stop his brows from arching in surprise. She gave him a cool stare. "Sorry about that," she said. "But I'm it."

He let his eyes take in a somewhat thin woman, a little shallow of breast under a white blouse, a compact figure, and a face with a wide mouth, sparkling brown eyes, and a small nose. Brown hair fell in a soft curl to the collar of her blouse and framed a face both innocent yet worldly wise, openly warm yet plainly skeptical. The contrasts combined to give her an intriguing pleasantness.

"You expected a wagonload of journalists," she said.

"Guess so," Fargo admitted.

Ellie Rogers' smile held a touch of ruefulness in it. "The Washington *Clairon* decided I was enough.

Besides, it's the kind of assignment they usually hand me,'' she said.

"What kind is that?" Fargo asked.

"Shit assignments," she said almost resignedly. "Far-off, strange, rotten assignments none of the other reporters want to take. So they send me. I'm the low woman on the totem pole, as well as the only one."

"Why do you take them?" Fargo asked.

"Why?" she echoed, lifting her voice. "Because I've no choice. I'm a woman and I want to be a journalist. A lot of people don't like that idea. So I take what they hand me and try to make them eat their words by doing a great story each time." She stopped abruptly, cast an inquisitive glance at him. "You with the major, big man?" she asked.

"Not really." Fargo said.

"You just a bystander?"

"Not really."

"Well, suppose you tell me what you really are," Ellie Rogers said. "While you carry my bags to the hotel." Her brown eyes waited, challenged, and he finally allowed a slow smile and picked up the two valises.

"Can't let you go away thinking I'm not a gentleman," he said.

She smiled back. "Not that you really give a damn about that," she said, and Fargo fell in step beside her.

"You're a sass-box, aren't you?" he said.

"A woman who wants to be a journalist learns to hold her own or else," she said, and turned through the doorway of the Dry Lake Hotel, a two-story, weathered structure that was really a glorified boarding house. She halted at the front desk and he set the bags down. Her smile was warm and quick. "You still haven't told me who you really are," she said.

"It can wait," he said.

"I'm expected at the major's for dinner. Come back afterwards," she said.

"Maybe."

He left her following the hotelkeeper to her room. He took the Ovaro and rode into the flat land and found a spot to watch the night slip across the countryside. He relaxed, and catnapped, and forced himself not to speculate on Danton Honegger and the Mescalero, not till he'd had a talk with Ellie Rogers. She'd come on assignment and he wanted to know what she had been told about the story she was to bring back. Maybe she could add a new dimension to the stupidity angle or help make things fit better.

Finally Fargo pushed to his feet, climbed onto the pinto, and rode to town. He took up a position in the deep shadows of a granary that let him see into the fort through the open front gate. His eyes were on the door of the major's quarters when it opened and Senator Thurston emerged with the major and Donna. Ellie Rogers followed and Fargo noted that she had changed into a white tailored jacket and skirt that gave her a crisp attractiveness.

The senator exchanged a few more words with the major and Donna and hurried on his way down the main street toward the hotel. Ellie Rogers lingered a few moments more with the major and left, too, walking briskly out of the fort. Donna went into the building with her father and Fargo waited till Ellie had passed him before he moved out of the deep shadows. She halted when she saw him, a half-smile touching her wide mouth.

"I wondered whether you'd show," she said.

"I can leave," he returned.

"No, no, you can't," Ellie Rogers said. "You promised to tell me who you really are."

He walked slowly alongside her. "Name's Skye Fargo. Some call me the Trailsman."

"That's who. Now, why," she said crisply, and his glance questioned. "You were watching when the stage arrived. You knew journalists were expected. Why are you here?"

"A man sent me to see if I could help the major with the Mescalero," Fargo said.

"A man?"

"General Howard Redfield," Fargo told her.

She was filing everything into a corner of her mind, he realized, listening with a true reporter's inquisitiveness. "Have you been doing that, helping the major?" Ellie Rogers asked.

"The major doesn't feel he needs much help," Fargo said.

"But you do," she said, and he laughed.

"You're good, quick and sharp," he said.

"That's right," she agreed brightly as they reached the hotel. "Quick enough and sharp enough to know you didn't wait for me tonight because I'm so ravishing. The woman in me wants to believe that. The realist in me knows better."

"You'll do." He smiled.

"That's not answering me. Why'd you wait?"

"Got some questions maybe you can answer."

She regarded him appraisingly. "I'll make you a proposition," she said.

"Sounds good."

"Not that kind, not yet, anyway." Ellie Rogers laughed. "When I do a story, I do it right. I want to understand the people, the country, the Indians. To do that properly would take months.''

"Try years, lots of years," Fargo cut in.

"All right, years. So I need a shortcut. You," Ellie Rogers said. "You help me. I'll help you. You tell me the things I want to know, I'll tell you whatever you want to know."

"Fair enough," Fargo said.

"But not tonight," Ellie said. "I've been riding that damn stage all day. I ache and I'm exhausted. How about we go riding tomorrow morning?"

"I'll be by," Fargo said, and with a bright smile she hurried into the hotel. He took the Ovaro back through town and had just passed the fort when the horse and rider came out of the darkness, dry-wheat hair pale under the moonlight. Donna halted beside him and he saw the glower in her fine-lined face.

"You get chummy quickly, don't you?" she said, and he waited. "I was coming out to look for you when I saw you going down the street with her."

"Anything wrong with that? Just being friendly to the press," Fargo said.

"That's Daddy's job. She's here at his invitation," Donna muttered.

Fargo frowned in irritation. "That doesn't cut any ice with me, honey. I do what I want, when I want, and with whoever I want."

"I don't like her," Donna said.

"Bitchiness or jealousy?"

"Neither. She was terribly sharp with her questions to Daddy," Donna said. Fargo recognized the protectiveness she'd drawn around her father.

"That's her job, asking questions," Fargo said. "Forget about Ellie Rogers. You said you came out looking for me."

"Yes," Donna said, lowering her eyes. "You were right about last night. I was awake at midnight, wanting you."

"Confession's good for the soul," Fargo said. "But making up's better. Let's ride."

She swung in beside him in silence and rode with him to the big bur oak, where he dismounted, pulled his bedroll down, and set it out. Donna watched him pull off his clothes, and when he was naked and had folded himself down onto the bedroll, she came forward, her lips parted, her breath a long, shallow sigh, her eyes moving across his body. He reached up, closed his hand around her waist, and suddenly pulled hard, yanked her down roughly. She came against him, her lips hard against his in an almost savage kiss as she pulled on buttons, clasps, wriggling herself free. In moments her skin was pressed against his, her legs lifting to wrap around him.

"Oh, please, please," Donna murmured, and lifted her torso to come down atop him, press herself over him. She cried out as he pushed up into her.

She moved her hips in a quick, pumping motion and he felt the sweet sensation closing around him, sensation that shut out all else but itself. He moved with her. Donna half-moaned, half cried, and her pumping grew more furious. She leaned forward, pressed the longish breasts onto his face as she pushed and rose, pushed and rose, with short, gasped cries in rhythm with each motion. When the little cries suddenly became gasped words, he felt her body grow tight.

"Now, now, oh, God, now. . . . ." Donna uttered, and Fargo arched his back upward, thrust high inside her. She trembled, then broke into a quivering, suddenly soundlesss moment, her hands, breasts, and upper torso pressed hard against him as her climax swept through her. Her moan, when it finally broke out, carried delight and despair as ecstasy spiraled away and she collapsed atop him, her legs straightening out to lie over his.

Finally, she slid over and lay beside him, the longish breasts with the dark-pink nipples falling to one side with languorous loveliness. Her hand came up and stroked his face, then down along his chest. "I want you to do something for me, Fargo," Donna Honegger said, her voice soft. "I want you to let Daddy carry through whatever he wants to do. Don't try to get in his way." Fargo turned and looked at her, a small crease touching his brow. "The senator is here, so is that Ellie Rogers. Let my father show off for them. Let him help himself out of this terrible place."

"You think it's that simple?" Fargo asked, and Donna nodded, pushing herself up on one elbow as she continued to stroke his chest.

"Yes," she said.

"Sorry," Fargo said.

Donna rose up straighter as a frown slid across her forehead. "What's that mean?"

"It means, sorry no dice, and sorry that's why you came," he said.

"That's not why I came," Donna denied, flaring at once. "I came because I wanted to be with you."

"But you don't mind trying a little pussy-bargaining to go along with it," Fargo commented.

She sat up very straight, her light-gray eyes narrowed. "That's a rotten thing to say," she hissed.

"Almost as rotten as it is to do."

Donna whirled, her breasts almost swirling. She reached out and pulled her blouse on, then quickly slid into her skirt as she stood up. "Now it's my turn to be sorry," she threw at him. "Sorry I came and sorry you can't ever believe anyone." Still tucking clothes in, she pulled herself onto the army mount. "Daddy's right. That General Redfield is out to crucify him and he sent you to find a way," she said hotly. "There's nothing wrong with a man trying to help himself while doing the right thing. I thought I could make you understand, that I could get you to care enough to try to understand, but you just want to make accusations. Well, I won't go along with any more of it."

"Guess it's collision time," Fargo said quietly.

She tossed the dry-wheat hair at him as she sent the horse into a gallop. He let her go, almost out of sight, before he pulled on his trousers and gun belt and followed. He stayed back, watched her, and scanned the night until she was at the fort. He turned away then and rode back to the big oak feeling a little less sour inside. Only a little less. She had wanted, had enjoyed. There was no lie in that much. But there were lies, someplace, somewhere, maybe more than enough to go around, and he had the feeling that time was running out on him. He swore silently as he settled down on the bedroll and went to sleep.

He slept soundly until the dawn sun came to wake him. When he'd finished washing, he dressed and rode back toward Dry Lake. He passed the fort and glimpsed Danton Honegger and Senator Thurston in the doorway of the major's quarters. When he rode on down the main street, he found Ellie Rogers waiting outside the hotel. She had on a brown, fringed buckskin skirt and a white shirt that rested on the shallow breasts.

Her smile answered his gaze. "I like to get in the mood," she said. "Helps me absorb things."

"You'll need a horse," he said.

"Got one at the smithy's. He's around back."

He followed her to the rear of the hotel, where a brown mare with white forefoot waited. She swung in beside him and he rode from town and led her out into the dry, hot, rugged country. He let her drink in the great sandstone formations, the spires and pinnacles of the high land. When she began to ask specific questions, she pulled a small notepad and a pencil from the pocket of her shirt and took notes. He showed her how the fruit of the prickly-pear cactus could nourish a man for days, how the giant saguaro could furnish water, and how to tell the cracks in the dry land that indicate water underneath someplace.

"The Mescalero know all these things. It's part of their being. Using the mesquite and the manzanitas and everything else that lives and grows in this land is as natural to them as using a dry hole is to a chuckwalla. Those rock formations and mountains are like your backyard is to you. They know every inch of them."

"Major Honegger says his troopers are a finely trained bunch of soldiers," Ellie said.

Fargo allowed a snort of derision. "They're young and inexperienced, and even if they were trained, they wouldn't be trained like a Mescalero. A Mescalero boy is made to sit in the sun until he can control how much he sweats. He's taught to hunt and track from the first moment he can walk. Before he becomes a man he's made to run miles in the hottest weather with a mouthful of water and spit it out at the finish to show he hadn't swallowed it. Young

Mescalero warriors are trained to stay in one place and dodge arrows others shoot at them.''

"You make them sound unbeatable," Ellie said.

"They're not unbeatable. You have to fight them with more strength than they have and with very sound tactics. Mostly, you fight them by containing them, not by fighting their fight. You can overwhelm them, but at your time and your place," Fargo said. "Field commanders who know the Mescalero are happy to keep them in line. The major wants to wage a pitched battle with them.''

"You don't think he can," Ellie said.

"Normally the Mescalero would avoid that. If they did go into a full battle, you can be damn sure they figure to win, especially against the kids the major has under him.''

"Major Honegger sounds pretty damn confident.''

"He does, and something stinks," Fargo said.

Ellie fastened an appraising stare at him. "You've more on it?''

"Later, maybe," Fargo answered.

"I'd like to talk to a rancher, get that background and viewpoint," Ellie said, and Fargo nodded.

"There's a man with longhorns north of here, saw the place when I was riding near one day," he said, and wheeled the horse in a half-circle. Ellie came along with him. When they reached the ranch, Fargo stayed in the background as Ellie spoke to the rancher and his wife. She was good, Fargo realized as he listened. She drew out both the rancher, a lanky, taciturn man, and his wife, and had them revealing inner feelings they probably never put into words before. Finally, with a gracious smile, she finished and rode away with Fargo.

"Thanks," Ellie said to him. "You've sure done your part. I got a lot of really great background material. Now it's your turn. Maybe we could find some shade first, though. Good God, I'm burning up."

He smiled, veered to the right, and led the way into a line of low hills. They turned farther up to where a collection of sandstone pinnacles formed a loose circle, and reined up alongside a clear pool of water in the center of the rocks.

Ellie slid from her horse, kicked off boots, sat down at the edge of the pool, and immersed her feet and legs. "Oh, does that feel wonderful," she murmured. She pressed her hands into the soil at the edge of the pool and arched her head and neck back as she lifted her face to the sun. The white shirt pulled taut against breasts that, while still shallow, revealed a lovely, long, swooping kind of curve.

Ellie cast a sly smile at Fargo as he watched her from the saddle. "You wouldn't like to go off somewhere and stand guard while I put all of me into this lovely cool water, would you?"

"I can stand watch from here," Fargo said. "Besides, I was thinking of cooling off myself."

"Would that be safe?" She frowned. "What with all you've been telling me about the Mescalero?"

"Nothing's absolutely safe around here," Fargo said.

"Including you, I'd guess." She smiled.

He smiled too and shrugged as he slid from the Ovaro. "I checked things out as we rode here. No pony tracks, no signs of anything. Besides, I'll let the Ovaro keep watch."

"The Ovaro?"

"There are ways," he said, and began to peel off clothes.

She watched him, amused interest in her eyes, and he put his gunbelt down at the very edge of the water. When he was almost stripped, he saw the amused interest in her eyes had turned admiration with a hint of something more. He stepped out of the last of his clothes and slipped into the pool, the water surrounding him at once, cool, refreshing, and he turned lazily, began to tread water as Ellie got to her feet. He watched as she unbuttoned the white shirt, let it still hang over her, undid the skirt, and with a quick, wriggling motion, shed everything at once and slipped off pink bloomers. She stood still at the edge of the water for a long moment and let him enjoy the sight of her, a gesture more of freedom than boldness.

The shallow breasts were not without their own beauty, he saw, the long curving line turning up at the bottom where each was topped by very small, very pink nipples that stood firmly on small, very pink circles. Ellie had a young girl's figure that fitted her breasts, slightly angular, flat-bellied with the width of her hips the only womanly aspect of it. And one thing more, he corrected himself: a very sizable and thick black triangle pointed down to smooth, nicely curved thighs and calves that quickly turned thin.

She stepped into the water, immersed herself almost up to her breasts, kicked out, and turned her back to float with lazy abandon. She glided backward through the pool, hardly rippling the water, with only the two very pink points sticking up over the surface. Fargo watched her swim around him in a wide circle, turn, dive, and come up alongside him, blowing air.

"Wonderful," she murmured, and he swam

alongside her and watched the water slip along the sides of her breasts and her torso. He dived below the surface with her and she instantly became a wavy water creature turning and twisting and then rushing to the surface, where she burst forth with a squeal of delight. He surfaced, saw her floating lazily, and swam to the edge of the pool, pulled himself out, and went to the Ovaro. He took a blanket from his saddlebag and spread it on the soil.

He took his gun belt, brought it to the blanket, and cast another glance at the Ovaro. The horse continued to stand with complete relaxation. Fargo stretched out on the blanket, rested on one elbow, and watched the young woman come out of the pool. She walked toward him, skin wet and glistening, the shallow breasts beautifully perfect on her. She came to the blanket, halted, and stood before him. Tiny drops of water clung to the curls of the dense black nap with shimmering provocativeness. He reached up, put his hand against the softly wiry triangle, and the little drops of water ran down his fingers.

"Oh, God," Ellie Rogers breathed. "I've never done anything like this, in the sun with someone I only just met."

"There's moment, time, and place," Fargo said softly, and pressed his hand deeper through the black, dense nap. Ellie sank to her knees in front of his and her arms snaked around his shoulders. He pushed still deeper into the curly nap and she gave a tiny shudder.

"Not just time and moment," she breathed. "You, something about you." Her arms came up, wrapped around his neck, and she fell over him, her wide mouth opened, hungrily pressed down over his lips. He was surprised to feel her tongue dart out so instantly and so forcefully, probing, seeking, caressing. "Oh, God," Ellie murmured, and the wetness of her body was smooth against his skin. He reached down, drew one hand across her shallow breasts and she almost leapt from his grasp. She half-turned, her head arched back, and a small cry spiraled from her open lips. Her hand grabbed his, held atop his fingers, and she pressed his palm down along the swooping curve of her breasts, back up again, and then down to the tiny, very pink and firm nipples. He drew his thumb slowly over each and her entire body quivered. His lips moved down to close around one nipple and Ellie screamed in pure satisfaction. Her hands closed around the sides of his face, pressing him down harder on the upward curves of first one breast and then the other.

She trembled violently as he sucked on the tiny nipples, gently clamped his teeth down on the soft curving bottoms. Now he pushed his face down across her flat abdomen, licking the still-moist smoothness of her body. "God, oh, God," Ellie cried out. She continued to tremble with pleasure, her body shaking as she responded to his touch, her entire being an explosion of tactile sensation. He moved his lips down into the dark nap and Ellie screamed out. Her hands were atop his head, pushing him down farther. "Yes, yes, please, please, iiiiieee . . . oh, yes, yes," she pleaded even as her hips rose, twisted, fell back again.

When his tongue touched the dark and secret place, Ellie almost leapt into the air. He heard her scream curl into the heat of the afternoon. Her thighs lifted, clasped around him, rubbed back and forth against him as she continued to moan and scream until suddenly her body grow taut. Her hips rose, lifted him with her, and the trembling became almost a spasm as she held in midair, her screams suddenly only breathy sounds. He felt her contractions, tiny little quivers added to the violent shaking, and knew her climax was all-possessing, all-consuming, with a violence that seemed somehow out of place for her thin, angular body.

Finally, with a wrenching cry, she collapsed onto the blanket and lay trembling until that too finally halted and she lay still, tiny beads of perspiration cloaking her body. He lay half over her and realized he had joined her consuming climax, swept up by the headlong rush of her ecstasy. At last, with a long sigh, she pushed up on one elbow and he saw a mixture of desire and awe in her eyes. "I don't understand, really. Everything just happened," she said. "Different than ever before for me."

"You sorry?" Fargo smiled.

"Hell, no." Ellie laughed and pressed herself against him. "Surprised isn't the same as sorry."

"True enough."

"In fact, I was wondering," she remarked, tracing a little invisible line across his chest with one finger. "About again, here and now. Would that be too dangerous? Would that be tempting fate?"

He smiled and his eyes went to the Ovaro, traveled to the high rocks around the pool and back down to the horse. Finally he brought his gaze back to Ellie. "It's be tempting me," he said, and closed both hands around her ribs, pulled her forward, and turned her on her back.

Ellie gasped at once in anticipation and he felt her thighs lift to close against his hips. She began to tremble the moment his body came against hers, and her wide mouth grew even wider in a smile of pure delight. When his quickly growing maleness came against her, pressed over the soft flesh just over the dense black triangle with its own fervid heat, she moaned and lifted her torso. He felt her hand come down, curl around him, and pull him to the opened portal.

"Yes, yes, take me . . . oh, Jesus, take me." Ellie twisted her hips from side to side, her thighs tight around him as she tried to envelop and consume, wanting only the feel of him filling her with ecstasy. He made love to her slowly and her hands grew into small fists that beat a tattoo against his back as she demanded more, harder, faster. Yet she cried out with delight at his maddeningly wonderful patience. But again, her tremendous sweeping ecstasy caught everything up in its absolute totality and he found himself hurrying with her as, quivering and gasping, she twisted and thrust under him.

He felt himself beginning to explode as Ellie's thighs tightened around him and the convulsive quivering spiraled through her. "Oh, my God, Fargo . . . ooooooh," she wailed, and the quivering ended in a long, spasmlike twitching, and as he climaxed with her, he felt the deliciousness surround him, the caress of caresses that consumed and flickered away so quickly.

He heard his own groaning sigh join hers as she collapsed under him, and he lay half atop her, his cheek against the softness of the shallow breasts. The senses exhausted, consumed by their own passion, lay dormant and allowed the sweet satiation of quiet warmth to take command. Fargo rolled over to lie beside her and he let his glance go to the Ovaro, saw the horse standing placidly beside the pool. He turned back to Ellie. She lay with her eyes half open, a contented smile edging her wide mouth. He rose, glanced up to see the sun going into the afternoon sky, and he pulled her to her feet. "Time to get out of here," he muttered.

Ellie pulled her clothes on almost reluctantly, but finally dressed, she climbed onto her horse.

"What'd you mean when you said you'd let the Ovaro stand guard," she asked as they rode down from the rocks.

"He'd scent an Indian pony or maybe even see one," Fargo said. "You watch a horse's ears. When they move, you know he's seen something. When they stand up straight, you know he's gotten the scent of something. Same thing goes for the way he stands, alert or relaxed."

Ellie swung in beside him as he began to lead the way down out of the rocks and he saw the sun had begun its slide toward the horizon. "No questions for me yet?" Ellie asked.

He had a grimness in the smile he allowed. "You care what kind of story you get?"

"What's that mean?"

"It means, do you want a real good story or does it have to be the one you came for?"

"I'll go with any story so long as it's good," Ellie said. "Why? Do you have another story? A better one?"

"Don't know but I might."

"Don't play games, Fargo," Ellie snapped.

"What's Senator Thurston doing here?"

"You know the answer to that. The major invited him. My newspaper, too."

"Not good enough," Fargo said. Ellie frowned at him. "Why'd he come? Why'd he accept?" Fargo asked, and Ellie continued to frown. "A senator gets an invitation from a major to watch him put down the Mescalero and he just up and comes? Why?''

Ellie's face crinkled and she stared away for a moment. ''I never thought about it that way, but it does seem a little unusual,'' she admitted.

''Is Thurston one of the senators who are big on Indian affairs?'' Fargo asked.

''No, not at all.''

''He say anything to you on the way out here about why he took up the invitation?''

''Not a word. He talked mostly about my doing a story that was bound to make the front page,'' Ellie said. ''He got to be damn tiresome about it.''

''I can see the major inviting a senator and the press. He's looking to show off. What I can't see is Thurston accepting. It just doesn't set right,'' Fargo said.

She thought aloud as they rode and the late-afternoon shadows stretched across the land. ''It does seem odd now that you bring it up. You've something definite you're wondering about?''

''Not yet,'' Fargo said. ''But I want you to do something for me. I want you to keep your eyes open, especially around the senator. I want to know about anything you see that's out of line.''

''I guess that wouldn't be hard,'' Ellie said. ''Except where do I find you?''

''I'll find you,'' Fargo said. ''But in case you've something special, there is a place. I'll show you.'' He put the Ovaro into a canter across the flat land and led her to the big bur oak on the hill that looked down on the road into Dry Lake. ''You just ride out of town, stay on the road till you reach the hill and the big oak. I've been bedding down here most nights. I'll keep to it.''

"Why don't you just take a room at the hotel?" she asked.

He let his lips purse as he considered the question. "Maybe. I'll see. Meanwhile, remember this place," he said, and went back to the road with her. Dusk had started to lower itself when he halted a half-mile from the fort. "It's best you go back alone. We don't want to seem too chummy."

She leaned from the saddle, circled one arm around his neck, and her lips pressed against his, gently yet firmly.

"But we will be chummy again, I hope," she murmured.

"Count on it," he said, and she carried a little smile of contentment with her as she rode away. She had been a surprise, Fargo reflected as he turned the Ovaro back toward the big bur oak. He was often suspicious about surprises, especially those that came wrapped in powder, perfume, and warm lips. But there was an openness to Ellie, a kind of brassy toughness that left no room for guile or indeciveness. Ellie could be on a collision course with lots of people but not with herself, Fargo realized, and he thought immediately of Donna. Maybe he could still get Donna to see her father without the blanket of protectiveness she had wrapped around him. If he could reach her enough to do that, maybe she could reach her father.

Fargo was almost certain the major was involved in something connected to his putting on a good show for the senator. But it was still possible that Danton Honegger was simply being incredibly stupid and full of totally unwarranted self-confidence. The possibility had grown slimmer and slimmer, yet he couldn't discount it entirely. He'd have to try once more with Donna, Fargo told himself as he reached the oak and slid to the ground. He set out his bedroll and undressed quickly to pull sleep around himself. He had decided to make the coming day one of long, hard riding. Maybe it'd bring him nothing but sweat and tiredness, but it was worth a try. Almost anything was worth a try now. The smoke had grown thicker but he still hadn't found the fire. And time continued to run out, dammit, he swore as he closed his eyes and pushed away further thoughts.

6

Fargo had been in the saddle when the first pink streaks of dawn began spreading across the sky. He rode the flat land and moved in and out of the hills near the base of the Guadalupe Mountains. He had spotted plenty of unshod pony signs and he'd circled away from small groups of distant Mescalero, made his way higher into the hills, and peered at the tree cover where he knew Coronado's camp lay. He stayed amid the rocks for the most part, hidden as he watched the activity near the camp. There was not a lot of it, he frowned, a few small hunting parties moving out and down to the flat land, another trio of near-naked warriors riding along the high ridges of the foothills.

He let himself edge as close as he dared in the daylight and spotted two braves and three squaws dragging a peccary through the trees toward the camp. He waited till the sun was in the noon sky without seeing any particular activity, and he finally drew back, stayed in the rocks and crevices until he was far enough away from the foothills to return to the flat land. He halted, let his gaze survey the land again and slowly sweep along the foothills. This was where the major would have to come if he expected to wage a pitched battle against the Mescalero. And they'd see him coming, of course, and they'd wait for him to move into the foothills before attacking. They'd not move against a full cavalry troop in the open land, where the soldiers' firepower would count the most. But even Honegger had to know that. Which meant he expected to go into the foothills to fight. Fargo spit into the dry heat in disgust. With experienced field commanders and experienced troops it could be done, he grunted. But Danton Honegger had neither, not in himself, not in his men.

Fargo spat again and started to turn the Ovaro in a circle. He stopped suddenly, his eyes narrowing to peer across the flat land, where he spotted three wagons racing hard in a straight line. He turned toward them and they slowed to a halt when he reached the first, a converted Texas cotton-bed wagon with bows and canvas cover. The other two were also converted Owensboros, he saw, a woman driving the center one with a man riding shotgun beside her.

"You got anybody with you, mister?" the man holding the reins of the first wagon shouted.

"I'm alone," Fargo said, and the man grimaced.

"We were hoping to find ourselves a half-dozen men," the woman beside him said. "Extra guns would set right good with us."

"Why?" Fargo asked.

"We ran into a powerful passel of Mescalero back a ways. I'd guess at least fifty or sixty," the man said. "They came out of the hills and we thought sure we were gone. But they rode right past us, didn't bother with us at all. It was as if they were in an awful rush to get someplace."

"How far back?" Fargo questioned.

"Straight west. They were riding hard," the man said.

"I'd guess you'll be all right," Fargo said. "Dry Lake's a few hours ahead." He spun the Ovaro in a half-circle and sent the horse into a gallop across the dry ground. Leaning forward in the saddle, he finally slowed when he spotted the hoofmarks fresh in the ground. The man had been right, he frowned. There had to be at least fifty or more of the riders. They were riding hard but strung out, a few bunched together but most following in pairs.

Fargo frowned as the trail suddenly veered to the left and he saw the Mescalero had turned southwest. They rode straight, not even a single rider going off on a side trip. This was no hunting party, nor a war party out looking for victims. They were on their way someplace with purpose and discipline. His frown stayed as he followed for another two hours, saw where they had slowed their pace but not their direction. They were going straight south, almost as if they were on their way to Fort Stockton just northeast of the Davis Mountains.

Fargo slowed his horse and pulled to a halt. He'd not be drawn after them any further. The day was starting to draw to an end and he'd not chase a band of Mescalero all over the territory. He turned the Ovaro back and let the horse slowly retrace steps. He felt the crease digging into his brow: uneasiness jabbed at him. Fifty or sixty warriors too much in a hurry to bother with three easy-picking wagons, suddenly racing from camp. Perhaps they were going to meet with still others. Perhaps, Fargo pondered. But they were still a powerful force on their own. And they were not out on a casual ride. It wasn't like the Mescalero to pass up a chance for a quick and easy attack. But these had. Something far more important waited somewhere for them. The uneasiness clung to him as the dark fell and he rode through the night, gave the foothills of the Guadalupe a wide berth, and rode on across the flat land.

The moon had risen almost into a midnight sky when he reached the big bur oak and dismounted. He had started to take his bedroll down when he spied the piece of paper stuck against the trunk of the tree and held in place with a pointed stick driven through it. He went to it, pulled it free, and tilted it so the moonlight could shine on it.

The few lines were scrawled in pencil, he saw and he read them aloud: "Don't you ever stay home? Come see me. Maybe important. Ellie." He shrugged, tore the note up, and swung back onto the Ovaro. He rode unhurriedly back to town, a quiet, darkened place now except for the sounds coming from the saloon as he passed.

He halted at the hotel, woke the elderly clerk behind the desk, and asked for Ellie's room. He climbed a single flight and halted at the first door at the top of the stairs, knocked softly, and in moments, Ellie opened the door a fraction, saw him, and pulled it wider. He slipped into the room and saw a lamp burning low in one corner. She had on a long shirt and nothing else, and she reached up to kiss him, her warmth instantly penetrating his shirt.

"I was disappointed not finding you," she said reprovingly. "Were you out playing with Donna Honegger?"

He kept surprise out of his voice with an effort. "What makes you think that?" he asked carefully.

Her smile was chiding. "I attended a briefing at the fort today with the major and the senator. Donna was there, too. I brought you name up. The major dismissed you with ice. Donna did it with fire."

"And you think that means something," Fargo said.

"I don't think. I know." Ellie laughed.

Fargo let anger come into his voice. "You call me here to ask about Donna Honegger?" He frowned.

"You think I'd do that?" Ellie returned mockingly.

"You're female."

She thought for a moment. "True enough, but I didn't," she said. "I asked you to come visit because I saw something last night."

"Such as?"

"That window overlooks the street. I stayed up late working and I happened to look outside. There was the senator, the major, and another man going down the street. The senator was holding a thin brown leather carrying case. They stopped at the bank and the third man took out a key, opened the door, and they went inside. I was still up a half-hour later when they came out, the senator without his case," Ellie said. She sat back on the edge of the bed.

Fargo, his eyes narrowed, gave voice to the thoughts that raced through his head. "Now, why would the senator, the major, and the town banker be going into the bank in the dead of night?" he murmured.

"Exactly what I wondered."

"Let's go see what we can find in the bank."

"Break into the bank?"

"Can't think of any other way to look around inside," Fargo said. "Maybe you'd best stay here."

"Hell I will," Ellie said. She rushed to pull on riding britches. "I smell a story and I'm going after it."

Fargo smiled, watched her tuck the long shirt in, finish dressing, and hurry out of the room after him. Downstairs, he moved along the dark street against the walls of the buildings until they reached the bank, a narrow, unimpressive building with the shades drawn on a wide window. The door was padlocked and Fargo stepped back to survey the structure. He ran his hand along the bottom of the window and saw that it fit tight, stepped to the side of the building, and found a brick wall.

"Damn," he muttered, and Ellie gave a faintly chiding glance.

"You expect you could just walk in?" she asked.

"I can get in. I'd like to find a way where they wouldn't know somebody broke in during the night," Fargo said. He strode around to the rear of the building and she followed.

The rear door was secured with an even heavier padlock, but there was a narrow window to the right of the door. He ran his hands along the sill and the frame before he noticed the bars set back inside the window, and he swore again. He stepped back, scanned the street, and saw the small pile of empty burlap sacks against the side wall of what seemed a storage shed. He hurried over and brought one sack back, folded it twice, and then wrapped it around the padlock. He placed the barrel of the Colt into the burlap and against the padlock and fired. The lock bucked and jerked upward, but the sound of the shot was only a muffled noise, and when he pulled the Colt back and unwrapped the burlap, the center of the padlock lay shattered. He pulled the lock open, put it carefully down beside the door, and pushed his way into the bank with Ellie at his heels.

The Trailsman halted inside, let his eyes grow used

to the almost total blackness, and finally made out only dark shadows that rose up within the blackness. "You start feeling your way along the right side, I'll take the left. Find a lamp," he said, and started to shuffle his way forward. Hands outstretched, he felt his way along a thin wall, came to what seemed iron bars rising straight up into the air, and knew he'd found one of the teller's windows.

"Got it," he heard Ellie call out, and a moment later a soft yellow glow spread through the blackness as she turned the lamp on low. The bank took shape: two inner rooms, a safe, and the two tellers windows behind iron bars. One wall was lined with metal file cabinets and he heard Ellie groan.

"We going to have to go through all of those?" she asked.

"I expect they'll have names on them," Fargo said, and took a step toward the files when Ellie cried out.

"There it is," she said, and he turned to see her pointing to a thin brown carrying case against the far wall. The case rested against a single cabinet with a sign over it that read:

Registry—Land Claims & Deeds

Feeling a surge of excitement inside him, Fargo strode to the file and yanked it open with Ellie at his shoulder. The drawer was stuffed with manila envelopes, a name in the top corner of each, and he rifled through the envelopes and felt the smile touch his lips as he came to one named with the name Thurston. He pulled it out, found it was fat with contents, and drew the papers inside out onto a small table nearby. There were ten individual sheets, he counted, each a claim to a parcel of land.

Ellie picked one up and scanned it, a tiny gasp coming from her lips as they dropped open. "He's filed claims to most of the territory around here," she said.

"So he has," Fargo echoed. "Once these claims are registered in Washington, the land will be his to sell."

"By God, that's it," Ellie said, and stared at him. "That's what he's going to do, sell the land back East at a fat profit, and I'm going to help him, dammit."

Fargo's smile was grim. "The major is going to chase the Mescalero into submission. You'll write a big, front-page story about it, and the senator will use it to show buyers how safe it is to settle out here. Honegger will get his promotion, the senator his sales, and they'll all be rich and happy."

"And my story will be the centerpiece. That's it. Everything fits," Ellie said.

"Not quite," Fargo said as he put the claims back into the envelope and replaced everything in the file. "You're leaving out the key piece, the Mescalero. They're sure as hell not part of this clever little scheme, and they're going to blow it into a cocked hat."

"I'm beginning to wonder. Didn't you say the major has been dealing with the Mescalero?" Ellie asked.

"I said his sergeant had been. Maybe he was working a deal of his own, or maybe he was on orders from the major. I'm not sure yet, but it still makes no damn sense," Fargo said. "I know the Mescalero. They won't make any deal that'd help the army."

"Maybe you're wrong there."

"No, I'm not wrong."

"Then maybe you're wrong about the major. Maybe he'll surprise you and do just what he says he can do," Ellie countered.

"I'd like to be wrong there, but I'm not," Fargo said, and pushed the file cabinet drawer shut. "Turn out the lamp and let's get out of here."

Ellie plunged the room into blackness and he felt his way back to the rear door, opened it enough for her to hurry after him. He replaced the padlock with care and stepped back. If no one used the rear door, it would stay undiscovered, he noted with satisfaction. He swung alongside Ellie as she started back to the hotel.

She turned to him when the reached the hotel, her hand touching his arm. "Seems silly to ride all the way back to that bur oak when you could stay here."

"It does," he said, and took her arm as she instantly scurried up the steps. Inside the room, she whisked her clothes off to stand naked before him, turned, and all but dived onto the bed, the shallow breasts bouncing. He undressed and came down beside her. Her mouth came onto his hungrily and she trembled instantly as his hand stroked down along her breasts. He shut out all the unanswered questions and let the pleasures of the senses take command. There'd be time enough to wrestle with the unanswered, with the shadow of deceit and death. Life was a thing of balances, the bad and the good, the sour and the sweet. It was impossible to turn away from the sour, and a sin to turn away from the sweet. He joined in Ellie's gasped sounds of delight and sank into the warm sweetness of pleasure.

7

Night still lingered unwilling to let the probing fingers of dawn send it fleeing when Fargo rose quietly. He smiled down at Ellie's sleeping figure. He'd try to keep her alive and safe. What they had learned at the bank was not an end. It was only a beginning.

He finished dressing and she suddenly woke, sitting up fully alert. "It's not even light out," she protested.

"It will be soon," he said. "I want to be out of here before. Remember, not a word, not a glance. You just go on as though you know nothing. Go through all the motions as before."

"When do I see you again?" she asked.

"When the time's right." He blew her a kiss and slipped out of the doorway. He hurried down the steps on silent feet, passed the elderly desk clerk asleep in his chair, and climbed onto the Ovaro. He rode quickly through the silent street, hurried past the fort, and saw the front gate open, the two troopers standing sentry. He grunted in derision. He had reached the flat land beyond the town as the sun began to slide pinkness across the sky.

He rode to the spring-fed pool where he'd gone with Ellie, undressed, and slipped into the water. Later, he dried with a towel from his saddlebag. He pulled himself onto the pinto again and rode slowly through the stone formations and emerged onto the flat land. He felt bothered, as though a big meal sat unsettled in his stomach. He had more pieces now, but the picture still didn't come together. He continued to ride slowly, a frown on his brow, and let thoughts move through his mind in their own idle pace. The images remained disconnected, disturbing and irritating. He found himself thinking again of the fifty or sixty Mescalero who had raced southward in such a disciplined, purposeful hurry. Did it mean anything? Was it connected to the rest? Somehow, he felt it was, but he couldn't find a thread. Yet it kept reoccurring just as Pecosito's words returned. The major and the Mescalero, Fargo grunted. It sounded almost humorous, the title of some minstrel-show song.

The major and Senator Thurston had worked out a mutually rewarding little scheme for themselves. It seemed perfect, a nice, neat arrangement for all concerned. Only there was no way in hell the Mescalero were going to let it work. Fargo wondered if his very first thoughts about Major Danton Honegger had been right. Perhaps the man was conceited enough to think he could pull it off. But Fargo found himself grimacing as the thought refused to take hold. There was something more, and it somehow revolved around the major. Dry-wheat hair and light-gray eyes swam into his thoughts. Donna might still be the key, Fargo reflected. He had to try to reach her again, make her see reality was not the same as disloyalty.

He turned the pinto toward Dry Lake and rode unhurriedly, letting words revolve through his mind. When he reached the fort, he saw the major outside, a map spread out on a wooden table that had been placed near his quarters. Senator Thurston and Ellie looked on as the major drew lines and marks on the map. Fargo's eyes found Donna nearby, half-watching and half-listening.

"I'll draw them out here," the major was saying. "And then my main force will attack. They'll be cut down if they try to fight, and they'll know it. They'll have to turn and run. I'll have a third platoon ready to come in from the sides and keep them running, those that are left."

Fargo brought his mount alongside Donna and his voice was hardly audible. "I must talk to you," he said. "Tonight, alone."

She answered without looking at him, her voice a whispered sound. "Come at ten. I'll meet you by the gate," she said, and he slowly turned the horse away. The major had finished his briefing and rolled the map up as two soldiers carried the table away.

"Most impressive, Major," Senator Thurston commented warmly.

Fargo saw Ellie walk toward him and he slowed the pinto when he reached the gate. She looked up at him with a studied appraisal, her half-smile holding an edge of cynicism.

"If at first you don't succeed . . ." she slid at him.

"Something like that," Fargo muttered. "She can help if she would. I've got to try to reach her."

"With words or something more?" Ellie remarked, still holding on to the wry half-smile.

"Don't be a smartass," Fargo said.

"It's called being a reporter," she said. "Getting the facts."

"It's called being bitchy," Fargo growled, and she walked away with the wry smile. He put the pinto

into a trot and rode from the fort as dusk lowered over the land. He came to the big oak, dismounted, and settled down against the trunk to wait. He let himself catnap and the night deepened until the moon told him it was time to make his way back to the fort. He rode slowly and approached the open main gate under the eyes of the two sentries. Once inside, he saw Donna waiting to one side and moved the horse toward her. She retreated into the deeper shadows and he swung to the ground beside her.

"I'm listening," she said.

"There's more to it than you know," he said. "It's all been set up for the senator to make a lot of money and your father to get promoted away from here. Only it can't work. The Mescalero won't let it. That's still the bottom line."

"Really, Fargo, first you accuse him of stupidity, then of dealing with the Indians, and now of some plot with Senator Thurston," Donna said.

"I can prove the last. I hope I don't have to prove the first two," Fargo said. He reached out, closed his hand around her arm, pressed gently, and drew her to him. "I'm asking you to talk to him. I think he'll listen to you. Maybe then he'll listen to me," he said. "At least make him wait some. Buy me some more time." The light-gray eyes searched his face, resentment, anger, and the seeds of uncertainty inside them, he saw. "You'll be glad for it, Donna, the rest of your life. Believe me," he said.

"I'll think about it," Donna murmured, and started to turn away. He pulled her back, brought her face up to his, but she refused to offer her lips and he stepped back.

"Think hard," he said, and let her hurry away. She went into the house through a side entrance and he waited till he heard the door close. He started to turn away when he stopped and peered down the dark shadows at the back of the major's quarters. He took a half-dozen steps forward, the frown creasing his brow as he saw the army mount tied up behind the building. It would ordinarily have been stabled by this hour, but it was all saddled and ready to ride.

Fargo backed away and the frown dug deeper as he climbed onto the Ovaro and walked the horse out of the fort. He went down the road, but only a few hundred yards, found a hackberry, and brought the horse around to the back side of the tree. He relaxed in the saddle and waited, his eyes on the road that led from the fort. The moon rose higher into the sky and he guessed perhaps an hour had gone by when he heard the sound of hoofbeats. The horse and rider came into sight moments later, passed him only a few dozen yards away, Danton Honegger's tall, lean, blue-uniformed figure unmistakable.

Fargo let the man ride on a few hundred yards before he emerged from behind the tree and began to follow. When he reached the first series of low hills, he turned and took the high ground that let him see the racing figure below with ease.

The major slowed his horse after another mile but maintained a steady, ground-eating pace. Fargo carefully hung back, and as the major moved past the rock formations and continued west, the Trailsman felt the crease in his brow set itself more deeply. The army mount, standardbred with Morgan stock, proved to be a strong, solid horse that showed no signs of tiring, and Danton Honegger passed the high rocks and continued on. When he turned slightly northwest under the pale moonlight, Fargo followed while he kept as close to the rocks as he could. Finally, as the major's horse started to move to where the land began to rise, Fargo heard his own muttered words. "He's heading into the Guadalupe foothills," Fargo breathed aloud, and the frown on his brow began to turn into a ball of disbelief in his stomach.

Honegger continued into the foothills. Fargo swerved to one side, moved up a sharp incline and down the other side so that if the major should happen to glance back he'd see no one. But the route was harder and Fargo felt the Ovaro beginning to tire. He let the horse slow enough so he could still keep the major's figure in sight, and suddenly he saw the army mount pulled to a halt. Fargo reined up, straining his eyes to peer forward. Suddenly four horsemen appeared atop a ridge. They came forward and Fargo eased closer. The four riders took definite shape, their almost naked bodies glistening under the moonlight, the Mescalero brow band on each one. They fell in on both sides of the major and led him on deeper into the foothills.

"I'll be goddamned," Fargo breathed, and felt the shock waves pounding inside him.

The four Mescalero disappeared into thick tree cover with the major, and Fargo spurred the pinto forward. Inside the trees, he heard them not far ahead, moving steadily through the woods. He moved a little closer as he swung in behind the five riders, the sounds of their horses easily covering that of his. He realized the frown of astonishment had become a permanent thing on his brow.

The Mescalero camp came into sight, a fire burning high to send its orange glow through the woods. Fargo halted, drew his horse into a thicket of trees, and swung from the saddle. He hurried forward in a half-crouch, circled, and halted on a mound of earth that let him see clearly into the camp just as the major rode in with his escort. The large wickiup at the far end opened to emit the bare-chested figure in the white, cut-down trousers. Fargo watched as Honegger dismounted and the Mescalero chief halted in front of him. Mangas Coronado's hawk-nose face neither smiled nor scowled, the small, slitted eyes showing only cold impassiveness. Fargo heard the major say something in Spanish. The Mescalero replied and the two men then disappeared into the wickiup.

Fargo dropped to one knee and heard his long, deep sigh of astonishment. He was there, watching, and still found it hard to believe what he saw. The Mescalero and the major, no glib phrase, no minstrel-hall joke, but reality, unbelievable reality. It wasn't possible. It couldn't be. Yet it was happening before his very eyes. The awe that churned inside him was joined by an icy anger. The sergeant hadn't been onto something of his own. He had acted on orders. He had killed Pecosito on orders. Danton Honegger was a lying bastard, that was certain, regardless of whatever else he was.

Fargo continued to stare in breathless disbelief at the camp and saw the other Mescalero settle down to sleep, a lone squaw tending the fire. He estimated close to a half-hour had gone by when he saw the two figures step from the wickiup. Honegger went to his horse, climbed onto the mount, and slowly began to ride from the camp. Fargo's eyes stayed on the Mescalero chief and he thought he saw the faintest hint of a smile touch the Indian's thin lips before he turned back into his wickiup.

Fargo waited and saw that the camp remained

quiet. He slowly moved backward, took the Ovaro's reins and walked away. He kept walking the horse until he was certain he was safely out of earshot of the camp, then he swung into the saddle. He could still hear the major's horse moving quickly through the woodland terrain and he made no effort to draw closer to the man. When he reached the end of the woodland and emerged onto the more open hills, he glimpsed the major far ahead, riding hard back to the fort.

Fargo let Honegger go on out of sight and kept the Ovaro at a slow pace as he rode through the night, the moon already moving down toward the horizon. The things he had just witnessed continued to stab at him and defy belief. He rode with disbelief and confusion as his saddlemates. His mood became increasingly grim as he rode the long, lonely path back to the bur oak, a kind of bitterness curling inside him. When he finally reached the big oak, he saw a horse to one side and a slender figure standing against the tree. He reined up and the young woman gazed appraisingly at him. "I was about to leave," Ellie said. "You look more than tired. Where've you been?"

"Dreaming, only it wasn't a dream. Imagining things only I wasn't imagining. Trying to believe something I can't believe," he said, and heard the bitterness in his voice.

Ellie frowned at his words. He swung to the ground and told her everything that had happened, biting out sentences in terse clusters. When he finished, she let a long breath escape her and he watched her wide mouth purse as she thought aloud.

"Quite a story, all right," she said. "I think you've thoroughly underestimated the major. It seems he's a very clever man. It's obvious he's worked out something with the Mescalero to make himself look good.''

Fargo's lips bit down on each other. "Maybe I underestimated the major, but not his cleverness. I underestimated his stupidity. I know the Mescalero, goddammit. They won't deal. Somehow, someway, they're going to slaughter him and his men. They'll outmaneuver him, outfox him, outthink and outfight him." He halted and saw her brown eyes studying him thoughtfully. "You don't believe me either, do you?" he grunted bitterly.

"I just wonder if maybe you could be wrong, Fargo," Ellie said calmly. "Maybe you ought to think about that possibility. I mean, nobody's always right.''

"True enough. Only I'm right about this. I don't know what Coronado is going to do or what he's got planned, but he's going to turn it around on the good major. You can bet your little ass on that," Fargo insisted angrily.

Ellie stepped to him, put her arms around his neck. "Come back with me. You could use a bed.''

"Thanks, but I'm staying here," Fargo said. "I told Donna Honegger to talk to her pa, that he'd listen to her. She said she'd let me know. I want to be here if she comes looking to help.''

"All right," Ellie said understandingly. "But what if she doesn't help? What happens next?''

Fargo shrugged. "I've no answers on that, not now anyway. But the major's going to have to tell you and the senator when he's going to put on his big show. You come find me the minute he tells you.''

"What if it's all too late to stop?" Ellie asked.

"What if there's nothing you can do but stand by and watch?"

Fargo made a harsh sound. "Then I'll come get you so you'll be alive to tell the real story."

She smiled, pressed her lips on his. "I'll settle for that," she murmured, and he gave her a hand onto the horse. He watched her ride away, followed her halfway back, and satisfied that she was safe, he returned to the big oak, laid out his bedroll, and was asleep in seconds.

He didn't wake till the sun was high enough to bathe him with its warmth. He washed and dressed at a trickling stream and realized he could do nothing to take the bitterness out of his mouth. Perhaps there was nothing to do but wait, as Ellie had put into words, wait and watch the tortured and twisted events go their course. No, he bit out silently. He couldn't just sit by and watch a brigade of young troopers ride to their deaths. He had to do something to try and stop it. Even a futile gesture would be better than sitting idly by.

His lips drew back as he thought about Danton Honegger. Maybe the only way to stop it was to stop the major from leading his men out. Fargo warmed to the thought. He'd risk a firing squad doing it, but Ellie knew the real story of what was planned. Honegger and Thurston wouldn't want that to come out.

Maybe he could make them both back down. That would mean Ellie'd have to kill the biggest story she ever had in her grasp, Fargo realized. But Ellie knew compassion. She wasn't the kind to trade lives for ambition.

He turned, climbed onto the pinto and started to ride toward Dry Lake and the fort. If he were going to go after Honegger, he wanted another look inside the fort and the layout of the officers' quarters. He rode unhurriedly and let thoughts revolve through his mind even as he scanned the distant terrain. But no brilliant answers exploded inside him, and when he reached the fort, the grimness lay on him like an invisible cloak. He had just entered the main gate and moved the pinto to one side when he saw Donna come from the major's quarters, her dry-wheat hair bright against a dark-blue blouse. She hurried toward him, light-gray eyes casting nervous glances around her as she paused beside the pinto.

"I want to see you, tonight," she said in a half-whisper. "We have to talk."

Fargo kept his face impassive, but he felt the stab of excitement inside himself. "I'll wait at the big oak," he murmured.

"No, not there," Donna said, and let herself seem to be admiring the Ovaro as she stroked the horse's head. "I don't want to be seen riding out. I'll meet you in the trees behind the rear of the fort. Ten o'clock."

"I'll be there," he said. She gave the pinto a last pat and hurried away. Fargo turned the horse and rode calmly from the fort, but inside himself he embraced hope with grim desperation. With Donna coming around to help there was a new chance, he was certain. He put the Ovaro into a canter and returned to the open terrain, riding toward the sandstone formations as he swept the ground with eyes that missed little. Unshod pony tracks appeared near the sandstone, fresh tracks with crisp edges. Three groups, not more than two in each group. They traveled west at a steady pace. Scouting parties that didn't scout, Fargo frowned, and he studied the tracks again. They rode as though they were measuring distances. He turned the Ovaro away and found himself thinking of the fifty Mescalero he had seen streaking south. They were on a mission, and fear sprang into his mind again. Why had Coronado sent to large a force from his camp at this time? There had to be a meaning, a connection.

Fargo found a place between the rocks of a small hill, settled himself down, and let time go by as he continued to scan the countryside. But nothing moved, no Mescalero warriors, not even a horned lizard. An ominous silence held the land. He shook away the chill that went through him in the heat of the day, pulled Donna and hope to the front of his mind, and closed his eyes to rest. When the day ended, he rode back to the bur oak and waited there until the night grew deep before starting for the fort. The moon was high in the sky when he reached the fort, made a wide circle, and came up behind the stockade.

A stand of smooth sumac started some two dozen feet from the wall and stretched back. He moved into the trees and searched the filtered moonlight for the pale gold of dry-wheat hair and finally spied it off to his left. He steered the Ovaro toward her. Donna waited, unmoving, until he reached her and swung to the ground. "I'm glad you're here," he said. "You're doing the right thing."

"I still think you're very wrong, Fargo," Donna murmured, and he felt the furrow crease his brow.

"Then why'd you ask me to meet you?" he said.

The voice that answered came from the trees nearby. "Because I told her to," it said, and Fargo spun, saw Danton Honegger's tall, lean form rise from the underbrush. "Drop your gun, Fargo. You're surrounded."

Fargo, his hand on the butt of the Colt instantly, half-turned and saw the circle of troopers stand up. Two were within a dozen feet of him, he saw, and he cursed silently. His glance took in Donna as she stared at the ground, her head bowed. He could blast away at least three of the troopers, he realized, but shook away the thought. Killing Honegger's young troopers would only make things worse for everyone except the Mescalero. But he'd be damned if he'd hand himself over to Honegger.

Fargo took two steps backward. "All right, everybody stay loose," he called, and dropped his hand from the Colt. With a sudden, lightninglike motion, he dived backward and to the side all in one motion. He hit the brush, rolled, slammed into the ankles of the nearest trooper, and the man went down, his rifle discharging into the air. Staying low, Fargo saw the other nearby trooper rush forward, and he came up with a swinging left hook. It landed high on the trooper's shoulder but knocked his rifle aside and Fargo's following right landed and the soldier went down. Fargo raced forward through the opening, swerved to race for the Ovaro when he skidded to a halt as a second line of troopers rose from the brush. The major had come prepared not to lose his quarry. Fargo cursed, yanked the Colt from its holster, and fired a volley of shots carefully aimed not to hit anyone.

They had the effect he wanted as four of the soldiers dropped down and another two dived to the side. Fargo raced forward, saw a young trooper rise up and rush for him. He spun, still stayed low, and brought up a looping left as the soldier reached him. It landed flush on the trooper's jaw and he went down. Fargo spun again, saw both the first circle and the backup line start to recover and close in on him. He raced to one side, then the other, tried to lead the blue uniforms into going the wrong way, but they came on, closing together as they did. He picked the nearest two and charged at them, saw both soldiers raise their rifles.

"Halt," one called out, and Fargo dived forward and low, hit the ground as the rifle shot passed over him. He got one hand out, wrapped it around an ankle, and yanked, and the soldier went down. Fargo started to rise and race forward, then the blow came down from behind, the rifle butt slamming into the back of the neck.

He felt the pain and the flashing red and yellow lights that went off inside his head as he went down. He shook off the flashing lights but felt hands seizing his arms and legs, taking hold of the back of his shirt. He was yanked to his feet; he shook his head again and stared at the major, who came up, anger in his imperious face.

"Put him in solitary," Danton Honegger hissed, managing a faint smile of triumph.

A trooper clinging to each arm and the others in front and behind, Fargo was half-pushed, half-pulled through the trees. He saw Donna standing to one side, her face shrouded with unhappiness. She turned away from his accusing glare. The troopers marched him into the fort through one of the two rear doors.

"Put his horse in the stables," he heard Honegger order. The soldiers marched him across the stockade yard.

His gun was taken from him and he was flung into a small cell with a lone window in one corner and a candle burning against the wall. The troopers left and he turned to see one slam a second door shut outside the building and take up guard, his head visible through the window cut into the door. The small alcove outside the cell held a toilet and a basin, he noted.

Fargo stepped back from the barred door and sank down on the narrow, hard cot against one wall. He swore silently at Donna and at the same time at himself. He had let himself believe that reason could overcome protectiveness, that her inner knowing could win in that collision course. He'd been wrong. He'd no right to let himself believe that. They'd taken the big Colt, but the thin, double-edged throwing knife was still inside the calf holster around his leg. He'd break out of here, he was certain, but he'd wait till the night grew deeper.

He lay with his eyes half-closed, counted off minutes, and knew that no more than a half-hour had passed when he heard the voices outside. He swung to his feet. The outer door opened and Danton Honegger entered the little alcove, motioned to the guard, and the door was slammed shut. The man took a few steps closer to the cell, a smile that combined disdain and triumph touching his lips.

"Donna told me you've been snooping around," the major said.

"More than she knows," Fargo said, and saw the major's brow lift. "I followed you to Coronado's camp," Fargo finished. The man's brows arched still further.

"You have been busy," Honegger muttered. "Fortunately, Donna believes me."

"I know what you and the senator have set up," Fargo said. "What do you think you've worked out with the Mescalero?"

"Think I've worked out?" the major said chidingly. "Your problem is you can't believe anyone is clever enough to deal with those damned Indians."

"Spell it out for me, just for the hell of it," Fargo said, counting on the man's desire to show off.

"The Mescalero will attack, only it won't be for real. But it'll look that way. My troops will go after them, split them into small parties, and chase them out of sight. They'll make it look good while they run. That'll be the story Miss Rogers will be putting on the front page."

"So the senator can sell all his wonderfully safe land," Fargo sneered. "What'd you offer the Mescalero to put on this goddamn charade?"

"A hundred army carbines. That was their price," Fargo felt bitter amazement. "And you agreed. Goddamn, I don't believe what I'm hearing. You gave them a hundred army carbines so you could make yourself a big hero in print and get promoted out of here. You've made it so the Mescalero can massacre every man, woman, and child in the whole territory. More than that, they'll start with you and your troop."

"No, they won't. We made a bargain."

"You are stupid. You really think they're going to hold to that? Jesus, you poor fool. You conceited, stupid ass." Fargo was half-shouting now.

Honegger's eyes were cold pinpoints of disdain. "They'll hold to it because they have to. I gave them the rifles, but they won't get the bullets until they've played their part," he said.

Fargo stared at the man and realized he was still draped in bitter amazement. "It'll be all right then if they turn the territory red with blood. Your little charade will be over. You'll be a hero and the senator will have his land claims ready to sell. That's all that matters to you. Good God, I don't believe this."

The major's smile came, filled with pompous smugness. "There'll be no massacre. When Coronado comes to get the bullets, I'll take him in, dead or alive. You see, Mr. Fargo, I've thought out every detail." He uttered a short, self-satisfied laugh as Fargo stared at him. "Please don't talk to me about breaking my word to a savage. An agreement with the Mescalero isn't worth honoring."

"You are a real bastard, aren't you?" Fargo said. "The only thing about this is that's just how they feel about you."

"Only I hold all the cards," Honegger said.

"No, goddammit, no," Fargo snapped. "I know better. I know Coronado. He'll beat you at your own game. Somehow, he'll outfox you, and you're too damn dumb to realize it."

"There's no way he can," Honegger said. "I hold the ace card, the ammunition. That's what you can't swallow, Fargo. My being more clever than any of you. Unfortunately, that's something you'll have to take to your grave. You know too much now. I'll have to arrange something for you." Fargo said nothing and Honegger started to turn away, paused, and looked back at him. "You've been getting friendly with Miss Rogers, I understand. I hope, for her sake, that you haven't told her any of what you've learned."

"Not a word," Fargo lied blandly.

"I'd hate to have to arrange for the senator to carry her wonderful account back posthumously," Honegger said, narrowing his eyes at the big man in the cell.

"Not a word," Fargo repeated. Silently, he cursed Danton Honegger.

The man turned away again and this time opened the door and left, the trooper outside pulling the door closed tightly.

Fargo sat down on the edge of the cot, let another half-hour go by, and rose to his feet. He walked to the cell door and pounded on it. He raised his voice in a shout and the soldier opened the outside door and stared in at him. Fargo pointed to the toilet and the soldier stepped into the room, closed the outside door, and held his rifle pointed at him.

"Get back from the door," the soldier said, a young man with an edge of hardness in his face.

Fargo moved back into the cell and the soldier took a key hanging on a wall peg and opened the door, keeping him covered with the rifle at the same time. He stepped away from the door and motioned with the gun.

"How about a little privacy?" Fargo asked.

"Do your thing and shut up," the soldier said, but he stepped back to the front door.

Fargo stepped to the toilet, undid his trousers, and started to lower the legs, but he let his right hand slip down to the calf holster. He drew the knife out, pulled his trousers up, and whirled as he sent the thin blade hurtling through the air. It hit the soldier's hand, ran through from one side to the other, and the man gave a cry of pain as he let the rifle drop from his grip. Fargo, dived forward, scooped the gun up in one motion and had the barrel pushed into the soldier's belly as the man stared at the thin blade still embedded through his hand.

Fargo pulled the blade free, herded the soldier into the cell, and slammed the door. "Wrap your kerchief around your hand," he said. "You'll be fine when they find you, come morning."

"Damn, mister, you'll never get away with this," the trooper said.

"If that hand keeps you from holding a rein, I might just have saved your life, sonny," Fargo said. He slipped outside and saw another block of two cells and an office. He stepped in and saw the pegs on the wall with his Colt hanging from one; he pulled the gun down and pushed it into his holster. When he left the building, he forced himself to stroll casually toward the stables. Even though the stockade area was mostly deserted, the men asleep in their barracks, the two sentries atop the walls scanned the interior as well as the outside of the stockade. When he reached the stables, he found a kerosene lamp glowing from a wall bracket. It allowed him enough light to find the Ovaro in a far stall, his saddle against the wall nearby. The other horses detected the presence of a stranger at once and grew restless. He quickly tossed the saddle on the Ovaro without tightening it and led the horse outside.

He halted a half-dozen feet from the stable and finished putting the saddle on properly. He had just tightened the cinch when he saw the door to the major's quarters open. He moved back into the deep shadows against the stockade wall as Honegger stepped outside with Senator Thurston, his voice carrying clearly through the stillness.

"I'm apprehensive about the Rogers woman," the major said. "Fargo says he told her nothing but I'm not sure I believe that."

"Christ, we can't have her going back with the real story," Thurston replied.

"No, we can't. She'll be in the wagon with you.

I want you to watch her closely. If she doesn't know anything, she should be excited, maybe afraid, sitting on the edge of the wagon seat watching what's going on. If she's just looking on calmly, we'll know that Fargo got to her and she knows what's really going on," Honegger said.

"If that's so, what then?" the senator asked.

"She comes back to town with you when it's over. You go through all the motions of being excited. I'll work out some way to take care of Miss Rogers," Honegger told him. "Fargo won't be around to give us trouble on that."

Thurston nodded and hurried away.

Fargo waited in the dark shadows, watching the major close the door and turn out the lamplight inside the room. He allowed another five minutes before he slowly walked the Ovaro out of the shadows by the wall, led the horse to the center of the courtyard, and swung onto the saddle. He rode casually through the open gates of the fort and turned into town. He drew to a halt in front of the hotel, dismounted, went past the startled desk clerk in two long strides, and took the steps three at a time. He knocked on the door of Ellie's room and she opened quickly with a frown.

"Where have you been? I came looking for you. Did Miss Indecisive make up her mind to help you?"

"She made up her mind, but not to help me. I've been sitting in the major's jailhouse," Fargo said. "Get dressed. You're getting out of here."

"Why?"

"When Honegger finds I'm gone, he'll come looking for you. He suspects I may have told you too much already. He won't take any chances on it now. He'll want you in his hands," Fargo told her.

"I went looking to tell you that his show is on for tomorrow afternoon. I'm expected in a wagon with the senator," Ellie said. "He'll know for sure something's wrong if I'm not there."

"Probably, but it's too late for him to turn things off now. He'll have to go through with his charade and hope you're watching someplace and he'll get to you when it's over," Fargo said. "He wants to have a whole brigade of troopers convinced they routed the Mescalero so they'll sign statements as to what happened. That and your story will carry off everything he and Thurston want."

"My story? Hell, I'll write the real story," Ellie said as she pulled on clothes.

"Not if Honegger can stop that," Fargo said. He waited as Ellie finished dressing, slung a small bag over her shoulder, and hurried from the room with him. He went to the stable with her to get her horse and started down the main street to the other end of town.

"Aren't we going the wrong way?" Ellie questioned.

"Don't want to risk passing the fort," he said.

When they reached the end of town, he turned the pinto in a wide circle as he headed west. As they rode, he told Ellie the rest of what Danton Honegger had admitted, and when he finished, she made a sharp, hissing noise.

"What a bastard," she said. "But you did underestimate him. He's been very clever. He pulled it all together for himself."

"He pulled death together," Fargo bit out.

"You're still sure of that," Ellie remarked.

"More than ever."

"You plan on finding someplace to hide me out?" she asked.

"No, there's no time for that. You're going with me."

"Going where with you?" Ellie frowned.

"To visit the Mescalero," Fargo said, and saw Ellie yank her horse to a halt, shock flooding her face.

"Are you out of your mind?" she cried.

"Maybe," Fargo growled. "But keep riding."

8

Ellie spurred her horse after Fargo as he rode on. "What in hell do you think you're going to do at the Mescalero camp?" she called out.

"I don't know," Fargo said.

"Then why are you going?"

"There's no place else left to go."

"You've something in mind. Don't lie to me, Skye Fargo."

"The Mescalero won't go through with it. They'll beat him at his own game. I know it, dammit," Fargo said. "If I can find out how, I might still be able to stop a massacre."

"You're grasping at straws," Ellie said.

"There's nothing else to grasp at," Fargo said bitterly, and settled down to concentrated riding.

Ellie rode in silence beside him as he set a hard pace until he reached the foothills of the Guadalupe. He slowed, moved to the edge of the thick tree cover, and turned into a thicket.

"We'll get some sleep. They might have sentries posted now. I don't want to chance it by dark," Fargo said.

They drew the horses deep into the thicket and out of sight before he set his bedroll down. He stretched out on it and Ellie came down beside him, folded herself across his chest, and was asleep in seconds. He closed his eyes and slept with her, all too aware that he might be able to do nothing. Yet he had to try.

When morning filtered through the heavy foliage of the thicket, sun spattering itself across the ground, he woke and put one hand over Ellie's mouth as her eyes came open. He slowly drew his hand away and his voice was a low whisper. "No noise. Move slow, breathe soft," he said and she nodded.

He used his canteen to freshen up and shared it with Ellie, then carefully made his way from the thicket and scanned the trees. Nothing moved. He beckoned her to follow as he stayed on foot and moved deeper into the foothills. He peered through the heavy foliage, drew deep drafts of air into his nostrils, and recalled his last visit to pick out markings.

When he caught the smell of burning embers and rawhide drying, he dropped to one knee and halted. His eyes narrowed, he scanned the forest on all sides, then motioned to Ellie to follow. They led the horses into a dense stand of hackberry. Fargo draped the reins over a low branch and crept forward on foot with Ellie at his heels. When he found thick-branched black oak, he began to pull himself up into the tree, paused, and gave Ellie a hand up as she started to climb. Once in the tree, she easily and nimbly followed him from branch to branch until he halted and pointed below and ahead where the Mescalero camp stretched out.

Ellie nestled against him on the thick branch as he scanned the campsite. The squaws prepared gruel over smoldering fires and Fargo watched the Mescalero braves emerge from the tepees and wickiups

He nudged Ellie when the tall figure in the gray-white cut-down trousers stepped from the largest wickiup, his hawk-nose face imperious, his slitted eyes surveying the camp.

"Mangas Coronado," Fargo whispered as one of the squaws brought the chief a wooden bowl of the gruel. The Mescalero leader ate slowly as the other braves went about their chores. Finally handing the bowl back to a squaw, Coronado returned to his hut and disappeared from sight.

Ellie, her eyes on Fargo's gaze as he scanned the camp again, saw his jaw grow tight. "You see something?" she whispered.

"It's what I don't see," Fargo murmured. "Only half his warriors are here. The fifty or sixty I saw racing south are still missing."

"What do you think it means?" Ellie asked.

"I don't know, but he's up to something."

"Maybe he's going to use only half his warriors for the major's show. Some are bound to be killed and he doesn't want to risk more than half," Ellie suggested.

"He'd just hold them back, not send them racing south hellbent for election," Fargo muttered. He sent his eyes sweeping the camp again. Some of the Mescalero warriors were carrying their army carbines with them as they moved around.

"They're waiting for the day when they can use them, I'm sure," Ellie said. "But if Honegger gets his way that'll never happen."

Fargo made no comment, but his jaw muscles throbbed as he continued to search the camp with his eyes.

"See anything that could help?" Ellie asked, and he shook his head. He felt her hand touch his arm.

"He might just pull it off, at least this part of it," she said gently. "It it so hard for you to accept that?"

He hissed his words at her. "I can accept anything he does. It's the Mescalero I can't accept. It's not like them. It goes against their character." He broke off further words as Coronado stepped from the wickiup and suddenly Fargo caught the sound of hoofbeats, lots of hoofbeats riding hard. The frown slid across his brow as he peered down to the south end of the camp where the hoofbeats grew louder, and he felt Ellie's fingers dig into his arm as the first of the riders burst into view. Fargo peered hard at the others that followed, a loose count of near sixty. He heard the curse fall from his lips. "Goddamn," he breathed. "Shit." He pulled on Ellie and pointed to the last half-dozen Mescalero as they halted with four horses in tow. Each horse carried an oblong box of wood strapped to its back, and the braves began to take the boxes down at once.

"What is it?" Ellie whispered.

"Look at the sides of the boxes," Fargo growled, and heard her short gasp of horror as she made out the stenciled letters that spelled out AMMUNITION. "The bullets, they got the bullets," Fargo hissed. "Coronado sent a raiding party all the way south to Fort Stockton, big enough to pick their moment, hit hard, and make off with the four boxes of bullets. That's more than enough to last them till they can pick up some more."

He turned to Ellie and saw the horror in her face as realization swept through her. "They're not going to put on a show for Honegger. They're going to attack, really attack," she said.

"And wipe out his whole damn troop," Fargo said.

"They never intended to go along with him. You were right all along," Ellie breathed in shock and awe.

"A fox will always outmaneuver a weasel," Fargo said grimly. He turned from her an saw the Mescalero quickly loading their carbines, shoving more bullets into their belts and pouches as they leapt on their ponies. Half-a-dozen rode out into the trees to form an advance guard. Two halted hardly more than a few yards from the big oak in which the two figures hid.

Fargo saw panic leap into Ellie's eyes; he placed a finger against his lips and she nodded. He stayed motionless, daring to take only soft, long breaths as he watched the rest of the Mescalero mount up, rifles in hand. Coronado swung onto an almost black pony with a white patch on the rump, then let his hawk-nose face scan the camp again. Squaws and a half-dozen warriors were left to remain behind as the Mescalero chief raised his arm, the loaded carbine clutched in his right hand, and motioned his warriors forward.

The entire band raced past underneath and Fargo felt the branches of the tree tremble. He watched the Indians ride on and let them disappear completely from sight before he began to climb down to the ground, Ellie hurrying after him.

"They're on their way to meet the major," she said as they pushed their way to where they'd left her horse and the Ovaro.

"I'd guess he's nearing the edge of the Guadalupe." Fargo nodded.

"Is there anything we can do?" Ellie asked, and swung onto her horse.

"Try to warn him." Fargo grimaced. "If we can

134

and if he'll listen. Let's ride." He sent the Ovaro forward, swerved his way through the forest, and when he reached the more open part of the foothills, he veered sharply to his left, drove upward, and stayed in the high land.

Ellie kept close behind him and he saw the Mescalero, close to a hundred strong, moving along below, letting their ponies keep a steady, even pace. He peered into the distance, but Honegger's outfit was not in sight yet. He spurred the Ovaro into a faster pace through the hills.

"I've got to get ahead of Coronado," he said to Ellie. "When I see Honegger's troop, I'll cut down from here, but I want you to stay in the hills. I don't know what'll happen and I don't want you riding through the middle of it."

"I can ride well enough," Ellie said.

He fastened a stern glance at her. "You're going to take back the real story of what happened here. I want you alive so you can do it," he said. She accepted his order with her eyes. He put the Ovaro into a gallop, aware that the horse could take the hill country, rock-filled paths, and still make time. He saw the Mescalero riding below as he came parallel to them and drew ahead. He kept the pinto racing through the rock formations of the foothills. He left the Indians falling farther behind. When he suddenly saw the distant figures appear below, he began to swing the Ovaro down out of the high land. Major Honegger's men took shape, riding in two columns of twos, the major and two lieutenants leading the double column. Following the column and rolling along off the left with six troopers riding herd, the wagon moved forward, a canvas-topped surrey with special side panels that let the occupants look out while being enclosed.

Fargo cast a glance behind and saw Ellie rein up, jump to the ground, and move behind a rock. He waved a hand at her and sent the Ovaro down onto the flat land. A glance to his right showed the Mescalero riding closer, and his brows lowered in a frown. Coronado had only half his warriors with him. He'd sent the other half into the high land to wait. Fargo cursed the Indian's cleverness. Coronado would draw the major's troops after him, seem to run, just as Honegger had outlined the plan. The major would lead his men in the chase with absolute smug confidence, and at the right moment, Coronado would halt, turn and pour his deadly fire into the troopers from the front while the second half of his warriors charged down from the side.

Fargo spurred the pinto into an all-out gallop. He saw the senator in the wagon beside the flash of dry-wheat hair. Honegger had brought everyone along for the show, Fargo swore. Why not? He thought he had everything completely in hand. He'd never listened, never believed, the price of conceit and stupidity. Fargo saw the major lift an arm, start to turn his men toward the onrushing Mescalero, and halt as he saw Fargo's galloping pinto.

"Fall back, goddammit," Fargo screamed. "They've got the bullets."

Honegger, his arm still raised into the air, stared at him with a frown in incredulity.

"The bullets," Fargo shouted as he reined to a halt. "They've got the goddamn bullets. He's outfoxed you, dammit."

"You never give up, do you, Fargo?" Honegger half-smiled. "You've some kind of an obsession about being wrong. Well, I'll deal with you later. Sound the charge, bugler,'' he ordered. Honegger brought his arm down and sent his mount into a gallop.

"No, goddamn, no," Fargo shouted, but his words were drowned out by the sound of the bugle. The two columns swept after the major and Fargo saw Coronado wheel his warriors in the tight circle and seem to run. As they did so, they broke off into smaller groups, and the major, brandishing his sword, ordered his men to do the same as they gave chase.

Fargo's eyes went to the surrey as it raced after the main force, the six troopers riding herd. He heard the bitterness and despair curled in the oath he flung to the winds as he turned the pinto and made for the surrey. In the distance he saw Coronado's men halt and wheel as the main part of the Mescalero force swept down from the hills. The air filled with a hail of rifle fire. Fargo winced as he saw a dozen blue uniforms topple from their horses, taken by surprise and caught in a cross fire.

Fargo drew his Colt and swerved from the wagon to race forward, firing as he rode. Two Mescalero fell from their ponies. Another pair whirled to come at him, and he flattened himself low across the Ovaro as he fired, his shots bringing down both the attackers as he raced between them. But the ground was already littered with blue uniforms as the Mescalero raced back and forth, outfighting, outriding, and outmaneuvering their foe who were still caught in the cross fire.

Fargo peered through the carnage to find Danton Honegger, and he saw the major on the ground, Coronado standing over him. Honegger's own sword pinned him to the ground through the center of his chest. Fargo saw the Mescalero chief step back and swing onto his saddleless pony. The Trailsman fired and the shot grazed the Indian's black hair. Coronado turned in surprise, saw him, and tried to bring his rifle up. Fargo fired again and the Indian ducked low as the shot grazed his shoulder. Coronado, low in the saddle, raced his pony away. When he was out of range, he turned to come back again, two of his warriors with him.

Fargo whirled, reloading the colt as he streaked for the surrey, where a dozen Mescalero had begun to attack. He saw the driver go down and two of the troupers. Three of the Mescalero also fell. The Indians were using their new carbines for the most part but not entirely, and he saw a trooper take three arrows in the back and fall against the surrey. One of the troopers leapt onto the rig and tried to grab the reins to turn the wagon, but he pitched to the ground as two bullets slammed into him.

Fargo fired, all but emptied the chamber of the Colt, and four of the Mescalero went down. Another shot brought down one of the Indians who had started to spin. Fargo saw the others give ground and race away to regroup. He reached the surrey, yanked the door open, and pulled Donna into the saddle with him. Senator Thurston came halfway out of the wagon, terror in his round face.

"You can't leave me here," he shouted.

"Just tell 'em you own all this land," Fargo said, and sent the Ovaro racing away. He didn't look back but he heard the senator's voice cursing at him until suddenly, with a gargled sound, it broke off. Fargo threw a glance back then saw the senator hanging

138

half out of the surrey, three Mescalero arrows jutting from his portly shape.

Fargo reloaded as he rode and pushed Donna down across the horse's sturdy neck. "Stay there," he barked. Pressed flat atop her, he fired at a near-naked horseman who swung toward him. The Mescalero took the bullet full in the chest but somehow stayed atop his pony for another ten yards before he fell.

Fargo glanced back to see the ground all but covered with blue uniforms, and he spotted two small groups of troopers, perhaps a half-dozen in each, racing away for their lives. A handful of Mescalero chased after them but quickly broke off the pursuit and returned to where the others had already begun to scavenge the dead soldiers.

Ellie had seen everything from high behind the rock, he knew as he raced the Ovaro east. She had too much sense to try to run for it until the Mescalero finished their looting and scavenging and went their way. But he couldn't leave her to ride out alone. She'd be thoroughly lost and could wander right back into the hands of the Mescalero.

He raced on and turned the horse left into the foothills when he was out of sight of the carnage. He rode into the rocks, slowed, and drew to a halt to let the pinto rest.

Donna slid to the ground and he noticed for the first time that she wore a full-length dress of deep green with a scoop neckline, both dress and neckline now torn in half a dozen places. The light-gray eyes stared up at him with the blankness of complete shock, but he offered no compassion, his face as if chiseled in stone. "You were right," Donna mumbled. "You were right all along."

"I wish to hell I hadn't been," Fargo said through lips that hardly moved.

The light-gray eyes searched his face. "He was trying to do the right thing."

"For himself."

"You feel no pity."

"Not for him," Fargo said. "Not a hell of a lot for you, either."

"Because I had faith in him?" Donna said, the light-gray eyes darkening.

"Because you wouldn't listen either. Believing is one thing. Being stupid's another. He was stupid on purpose. You were stupid out of loyalty. Comes out the same way," Fargo said. "Get on the horse."

"You sure you wouldn't prefer I walk back?" Donna asked tartly.

"I'd let you if I had the time," Fargo said. He reached down and pulled her into the saddle in front of him. He put the pinto into a gallop as he stayed in the hills, slowed when he neared the place where he'd left Ellie, and peered down at the bottom of the rocks. The last of the Mescalero were receding into the distance and the silence of death had already begun to lower itself over the land. Still in the rocks, he moved forward carefully, his eyes scanning the terrain, but nothing moved. The Mescalero had had their victory, an almost total one, and they were eager to return to camp for the victory celebration that would surely take up the night. He spotted the movement amid the rocks below and saw Ellie appear, leading her horse forward, and he moved down at once. She heard him, spun, and he saw the relief flood her face when she saw him. He halted, slid from the Ovaro with Donna, and Ellie clasped him to her.

"God, I was so afraid. I watched it all. I thought they'd add you to the others," she said.

"They tried," Fargo said.

Ellie stepped back and her brown eyes blinked as she spoke. "It was terrible to hide there and watch, see it all happening. I wanted to stand up and shout, tell them to stop. I've never felt so helpless."

Fargo's gaze went past her to the land below. The bodies that lay strewn across the land were mostly naked now, uniforms, boots, guns, and watches, underwear, and gold chains, everything stripped away and carried off. All of it would be used by the conquerors, some of it worn, some of it traded, and some kept as trinkets, souvenirs of victory and power.

"I want to find him," Donna's voice cut in. "I want to take him back with me."

"No," Fargo said harshly, and saw her lower lip tremble.

"Why are you being so cruel?" Donna asked. "To get back at me?"

"He led his men here to their deaths. He stays here with them. That's not being cruel. That's being kind, more so than he deserves," Fargo said. "Get in the saddle."

"She can take my horse," Ellie cut in quickly. "I'll ride with you." Not waiting for an answer, she swung up onto the Ovaro with a quick, lithe motion and Fargo held his smile as he climbed into the saddle behind her.

Donna pulled herself onto the brown horse and fell in step alongside him as he started down the rocky passages to the base of the foothills. "Are they just going to be left out here for the buzzards?" she asked as she rode beside him onto the flat land.

"I don't expect there are enough troopers left at the fort for a proper burial party. It'll have to wait till replacements come from Fort Stockton," Fargo said. "It's not right, but that's how it is. Life's not right. It just is." He put the Ovaro into a trot and it was nearing dusk when they reached the fort. The front gate was shut, he saw, and it opened only when the two sentries atop the stockade wall recognized Donna. He rode inside with her and a young lieutenant hurried to him as Donna slid from the horse and walked into the major's quarters without a glance back.

Fargo fastened the young lieutenant with a long, piercing stare. "You were there. You're one of those that got away," he said.

"How'd you know?" the lieutenant asked.

"It's in your eyes. It'll always be there," Fargo said. "How many men do you have left here?"

"Maybe twenty," the young officer said.

"You in charge?" Fargo asked, and the man nodded.

"First Lieutenant Henry Ridder," he said. "In charge of getting the hell out of here."

"To where, Lieutenant?" Fargo asked.

"To Fort Stockton. They've got to send replacements back with us. We can't hold this place with twenty men if the Mescalero attack."

"No, you can't, but they won't be attacking tonight," Fargo said. "But I will."

"Come again?" The Lieutenant frowned.

"I have to destroy all the rest of that ammunition and as many of the carbines as possible. Without the ammunition they can't go on the kind of rampage that will massacre everybody in the territory," Fargo said.

"You? How can you do that alone?" Ellie cut in.

"Alone is the only way. No raiding party will get close enough," he told her. "You should know that by now, honey," he added, and she nodded unhappily. He turned back to the lieutenant. "I'll need a sack of gunpowder and dynamite, say twelve sticks," he said.

"We have both in the supply shed," the trooper said, turned, and hurried away while Fargo met Ellie's sober stare.

"You've done enough. Let it go," she said.

"Everything was too little and too late. I'm the only one with a chance to turn it around, a last chance," Fargo said. "If I don't take it, a lot of people will pay the price."

Her arms reached out to encircle his neck. "I'm afraid," she murmured.

"You go write that story," he told her.

"I want you alive at the end of it," Ellie said.

"That makes two of us." He grinned and her lips clung to his until the lieutenant reappeared. She hurried away and Fargo put the sack of gunpowder over the saddle horn and the dynamite against the rain slicker in saddlebag.

"We'll wait for you to get back," Lieutenant Ridder said.

"Give me two days at the outside," Fargo said. "If I'm not back by then, hightail it to Fort Stockton, and good luck to you."

"Good luck to you, mister," the Lieutenant said gravely.

Fargo rode slowly out of the fort in the gathering twilight. He headed out along the road, turned onto the flatland, and rode west. He didn't hurry the horse. He wanted the pinto with plenty of reserve energy when the time came. But when he turned into the low hills and the night had fallen, he concentrated on listening to the sounds of the night. He heard the slithering of a sidewinder's distinctive motion, caught the scurry of a band of night lizards, and heard the cry of a red wolf in the distance. But the frown crossed his brow as he turned into the rocks of the low hills. He was being followed. He'd caught the sound of a horse's hooves. He'd have picked it up sooner had he not been straining his ears forward for sounds of a Mescalero sentry. He pulled the pinto behind a tall slab of stone, drew his Colt, and waited.

The horse and rider appeared through the darkness, moving slowly, plainly following his tracks. "Damn you, Ellie Rogers," Fargo muttered aloud, and suddenly, as the rider increased speed, followed a clear track left by the pinto, he heard his gasp of surprise as he saw the dry-wheat hair pale in the moonlight. He let her come closer before he emerged from behind the rock and saw her jump in surprise.

"What the hell are you doing out here?" he growled.

"I want to kill that Mescalero chief myself," Donna said tersely. "I want Coronado. He killed my father. He broke his word to him."

"Which was exactly what your father was planning to do to him," Fargo commented.

Donna's eyes shot light-gray fire. "You dare to defend that savage?"

"Not defending, just setting out the truth of it," Fargo said.

Donna looked away, her lips a thin line. "Doesn't change things. I want him," she said, and moved her arm to reveal the big Remington .44 stuck into the waistband of her Levi's.

"All you'll do is get in my way," Fargo said. "My only chance is to do it alone. I can't wet-nurse you."

"You don't have to wet-nurse me," Donna said. "You do your things. I'll just wait to do mine."

"No, goddammit!"

"I'm here. I'm going along," she said. "Or maybe you'd like to tie me up and leave me here?"

"I'm thinking about it," he growled, turned away, and cursed. "There's no time to take you back or I'd sure as hell do it," he said.

"Why is time so important? Why'd you have to come back tonight?" Donna questioned.

"They'll be holding their victory celebration tonight. They'll have the ammunition and the carbines in one spot so they can dance around them and offer their thanks to the great spirits," Fargo said. She understood and nodded with a blink of her eyes. "Dammit," Fargo bit out. "One wrong move and I will leave you."

Donna fell in behind him in silence as he moved deeper into the hills, steered the pinto through the thick trees. Finally they heard the Mescalero camp, the drums first, then the chanting. Soon they saw the soft-orange glow of the firelight. He moved closer before he slid from the horse, and Donna did the same. He dropped the reins over a branch and motioned for her to stay close behind him as he pushed silently and carefully through the trees.

The camp came into sight, two fires burning and the edges of the area crowded with the braves and squaws watching the dancers. Fargo dropped to one knee and Donna came beside him, her hand resting against his leg.

"This is going to be my last visit here," Fargo said. He hoped he'd not be right the wrong way. His eyes focused on the circle in the center of the camp between the fires. The boxes of ammunition had been stacked there and most of the carbines placed around the boxes. He grunted silently in satisfaction and watched the line of dancers parading around the ammunition boxes and rifles.

Each carried a wand and was bare to the waist with an almost floor-length, buckskin-fringed hide skirt decorated with tribal markings covering his legs. Each dancer wore a black cloth mask, atop which an elaborate headdress rose into the air. "Devil dancers," Donna murmured, "I've seen drawings of them."

"No, not devil dancers. That's a white man's mistake," Fargo whispered. "They're mountain-spirit dancers, sometimes called Gan dancers. They act out the parts of Apache gods, and in doing that they give thanks to the different gods for their victory."

Donna's gaze followed his as he watched the Gan dancers move around the ammunition boxes and the rifles in a loose circle, bowing their ornate headdresses as they danced and stomped their feet in a kind of broken rhythm. Each time they made half the circle, a squaw would step forward and offer the dancers a bowl and each dancer would pause to drink from the bowl. Fargo noted other, smaller wood bowls being passed around among the other warriors who looked on.

"Peyote," Fargo hissed. "It gives them visions, gets them dancing harder, and eventually it puts them into a trance and then a sleep. We'll wait some. It's already starting to have its effect." He leaned against the trunk of a young black oak as he remained on one knee.

Donna sank down on the mossy soil and put her head back. The long curve of her breasts pulled against the dark-blue shirt she wore and she somehow managed to look delicately entrancing as he let his eyes linger on her. A slow smile touched her lips.

"You're remembering, aren't you?" she murmured.

"And being sorry."

"About what?"

"Being right about collision courses."

The smile faded and she suddenly looked terribly sad. "I am too. I wanted him to do something right this time. I wanted it so much that I stopped seeing, or listening, or thinking."

"It's history now, and you're still being wrong. Being here is wrong. He doesn't deserve being avenged," Fargo said.

The sadness stayed in her eyes as she stared back. "You've no forgiveness in you, have you?"

"Not enough for a hundred troopers cut down," he said. "Not enough for selfish stupidity." He turned away from the resentment that came into her eyes, and listened to the sounds coming from the Mescalero camp. The laughing and chanting had died down almost completely and the drums were only desultory eruptions now. He rose and peered through the trees to see that most of the mountain-spirit dancers had collapsed in a half-circle around the ammunition boxes. A few were already in a trancelike sleep while the others moaned individual chants.

Fargo's gaze went to the rest of the camp and he

saw at least twenty-five of the Mescalero braves passed out on the ground. Others were settling down to sleep in the open and still others were disappearing into the tepees and wickiups of the encampment. He found the Mescalero chief standing in front of his wickiup, surveying the camp, his hawk-nose face wreathed in triumph. Finally Coronado went into his wickiup and Fargo rose, went to the Ovaro, and returned with the small sack of gunpowder slung over one shoulder and the dynamite sticks stuck into his belt.

He started down the small incline toward the camp, Donna at his heels. When he reached the bottom level, he halted, grateful that the trees came to the very edge of the camp. "This is where you get off," he whispered to Donna, and he motioned for her to stay. He put the sticks of dynamite down on the ground at her feet and turned to the camp where the boxes of ammunition lay directly in front of where he crouched. A narrow path was open to the boxes, he saw, with half-drugged and sleeping Mescalero on either side of it. He started forward, swinging the sack of powder from his shoulder and pulling the top open. Moving in a crouch, he began to lay a trail of gunpowder along the ground toward the ammunition boxes and the rifles alongside them. He grimaced as he came within inches of the Mescalero, froze as one of the masked figures stirred, half-lifting his head, and then fell back into his trance again.

Fargo skirted the two braves and a young squaw as he continued to lay the trail of gunpowder. He had only another dozen feet to reach the ammunition boxes when two of the Mescalero sat up, suddenly alert. Fargo dropped prone on the ground and cursed silently as the two Indians peered past the ammunition, turned halfway toward him, and lay back down again. Half of the camp was in a stupor from the peyote juice, but half had stayed sober and fully alert, he had to remember. He started to crawl forward again, scattering the trail of gunpowder a little farther, when another of the Mescalero sat up, a tall, thin figure who rose to his feet and walked to one of the fires, where he stood quietly and gazed into the embers. Fargo had flung himself flat on the ground again and he watched the Indian finally turn and walk a half-dozen yards to find another place to lie down. But suddenly the Mescalero still between him and the ammunition were all restless. He saw a squaw sit up, lie back down, but stay awake, and two more of the men toss and turn where they lay.

He began to crawl backward on his belly, moving along the ground next to the trail of gunpowder he had yet to complete. When he reached the trees, he told Donna, "I've got to wait for them to settle down again. It's only another few feet, dammit."

Minutes seemed to drag by with infuriating slowness and he guessed a half-hour had passed when the Mescalero seemed to have quieted down again. He started to crawl forward again, moving more quickly this time as he followed alongside the powder trail. He half-jumped, half-stepped over one of the peyote-drugged forms before dropping to a crouch as he reached the place where he'd stopped putting down the gunpowder. He started forward carefully again, and he'd put down perhaps another foot of gunpowder when he saw three of the Indians come awake.

With a silent curse, he flung himself prone on the ground again, turned his face on its side so he could see forward. The three Mescalero exchanged grunted remarks and one stood up and slowly turned in a complete circle. Fargo's hands stole to the butt of the Colt at his side. If he were spotted, there'd be nothing left but to try to escape with his skin, he realized. And he'd be damn lucky to do that, he added grimly. But the Mescalero's eyes searched the distance and he passed over the forms on the ground nearby. Finally he finished his slow circle, folded himself back down on the ground, and he exchanged further words with the other two. They'd not return to sound sleep soon, Fargo swore as he began once again to inch his way backward alongside the trail of gunpowder. He accidently brushed against one of the half-drugged figures and the man moved, moaned, but his eyes stayed closed and Fargo crawled on. He reached the edge of the camp again, faded back into the trees, and met Donna's eyes.

"You were lucky twice," she murmured. "You won't keep on being lucky."

He grimaced at the truth in her words. "And all of this won't mean a damn thing if I can't lay the gunpowder up to the ammunition boxes. Another lousy few feet, less than a dozen now," he muttered.

"You think they hear you?" Donna asked. "That seems impossible."

"It's not impossible, but it's sensing more than hearing. A rabbit doesn't hear the hawk but he often senses it," Fargo told her. "Now that their senses are awake and alert, it'll take even more time before I can try again."

"How much time do we have?" Donna asked, and Fargo winced at the question. The moon had begun to slide toward the horizon long ago. Dawn would put an end to the entire plan, he knew.

"I'm going to have to try again," he said, and his eyes were on the figures strewn across the ground near the ammunition boxes. They had settled into silence, at least. The apprehension in Donna's face was echoed by the clamminess of his hands, he realized as he left the treeline and started forward again. He crawled this time, inching his way forward in silence. Again he reached the spot where his trail of gunpowder halted. He began to sprinkle more from the sack when the nearest Mescalero spoke to his sleeping companions. One of the others answered, a dialect Fargo didn't understand. But he did understand one thing: they were awake, and he lay flat and unmoving as the Indians continued to talk in short, guttural exchanges. He looked at the distance still to be covered to reach the ammunition. Six feet, maybe eight, he estimated. Six feet that spelled failure if he didn't reach it, and six feet that spelled death if he tried.

He swore silently in bitter helplessness and frustration. One of the nearer Indians sat up and gazed across the camp, and Fargo heard others in the distance stir, exchange words. Restlessness could be like a silent wind, he knew, reaching out in some mysterious way to touch others. He waited and finally began to bitterly crawl backward again, cursing inwardly every inch of the way.

Donna was there when he reached the trees and lifted himself to one knee.

"We're running out of time," he muttered. "The ones not on the peyote are too alert now. What I need is a diversion, a cougar or a herd of mule deer, anything to draw their attention to the other side of the camp so's I can put down that last six feet of gunpowder."

"You have your diversion," Donna said, and he turned, stared at her, and saw the light-gray eyes stay steady. "I'll work my way to the other side of the camp. I'll draw their attention."

"It could mean the end of the trail for you," Fargo said. She only shrugged. "Trying to make up for what Daddy did?" She ignored his words and waited. It would work, he felt certain, perhaps the one last chance for success. He'd no right to refuse her offer. Too many lives depended on these precious moments. "Go ahead," he murmured. "But when they come at you, you turn tail and run. Come back around to here."

She nodded and in her eyes he saw that she understood his words held more hope than reality. She turned without another word and began to move silently through the trees to circle the camp.

Fargo stayed on one knee, the sack in his hand, and waited, his eyes peering across the camp to the other side. She circled carefully and took time that seemed a century, and suddenly he spied her almost opposite where he was on the other side of the camp. Dry-wheat hair shining pale under the moon, she stepped forward, walking straight into the camp.

Fargo saw two Mescalero leap to their feet as Donna halted. They set up an instant alarm and others came awake. Still more emerged from their teepees and Donna stood still, ghostlike in the last of the moonlight. Fargo saw the Mescalero in front of him rise, wakened by the murmurs of voices, all except those still drugged. The Mescalero crowded together in a half-circle to stare at her, uncertain and surprised at this figure with the dry-wheat hair that had suddenly appeared at the edge of their camp. Fargo saw Coronado, wakened by the noise, step from his hut and walk toward the others. They were all on the other side of the camp, their backs to him, Fargo saw, and he ran forward, no attempt to crouch now. He reached the end of the gunpowder trail, emptied the rest of the sack along the final six feet, and sprinkled the last of it atop the ammunition boxes. He tossed the sack down and raced back to the beginning of the gunpowder, knelt, struck a match, and tossed it on the dark powder trail, which flared up at once.

With a hissing sound the gunpowder blazed up, raced its way forward along the almost straight trail he'd laid down. It took but seconds to reach the boxes of ammunition, and Fargo half-turned away, anticipating the explosion. It took another half-dozen seconds, but when it did it filled the camp with the staccato roar of bullets exploding in a cacophony of sound that grew only louder as smaller explosions flew off in all directions. He saw the Mescalero whirl and heard their cries of astonishment. He glimpsed Donna racing back into the trees, but two braves had detached themselves from the others to go after her.

The shattered, exploded ammunition boxes were only a pile of splintered wood, their contents vanished. Most of the army carbines that had been stacked against them were blackened and twisted. The main body of the Mescalero were beginning to recover from their first shock, and he saw them start to move toward the wisps of smoke that rose from the exploded boxes. Coronado was the first to approach, but in his face there was more rage than shock.

Fargo spun as Donna came crashing through the trees and he saw the two Mescalero right behind her. One dived forward, seized her wrist as the second one raced past. Fargo drew the Colt and fired in one blur of motion. The Indian went down, his bare chest suddenly erupting in red. The one holding Donna let go of her, crouched, and drew his tomahawk. Fargo cast a quick glance at the camp where the shot had brought the others to a halt for a moment. They'd go into a charge, he knew, and he met the Mescalero with the tomahawk with two shots that tore the man's midsection into a gaping hole.

"Get your horse," he yelled at Donna as he lighted the first stick of dynamite. He flung it directly into the camp as the Mescalero started toward him, and he didn't wait to see where it landed as he turned and raced for the pinto. He leapt onto the horse, the dynamite in his belt. He lighted another stick and tossed it to his right, threw another one to his left as he was certain they'd spread out to come after him. "Ride," he yelled at Donna, and sent the Ovaro into a half-gallop through the forest. The sound of the first explosions had died away and he glanced back to see the Mescalero starting after him again, breaking into smaller groups.

He kept riding, waited, lighted two more sticks of dynamite, and tossed them back. He watched them explode and saw at least a half-dozen of his pursuers spiral into the air. But most of the camp had come awake and still others came charging. A number had taken their ponies. The tree cover slid to an end just as dawn streaked the sky, but the Mescalero had gathered themselves enough to properly charge after him. Donna was a few paces behind as he reined to a halt where the rocky terrain started. When the Mescalero appeared, he let them see him. They swerved after him immediately and he scanned the onrushing horsemen. Coronado was not among them, but the chief hadn't been killed, Fargo swore. If he had, the others wouldn't be in hot pursuit. He waited a few seconds more before lighting another stick of dynamite and tossing it at the charging Mescalero. They saw it arc through the air and tried to turn their ponies aside. But the space was too small and the dynamite exploded in their midst. Screams of pain and flying bodies filled the air.

Fargo had already sent the Ovaro racing forward. He swerved down through the rocky terrain of the foothills, glanced back at Donna, and yanked his horse to a halt. She wasn't there, he saw, and he raced back a dozen yards and still didn't see her. He was at the spot where the rocks lay with Mescalero draped over them and the smell of the dynamite still lingered in the air. She had stopped there with him he cursed as his eyes scanned the dry rocky terrain. She had stopped and turned up into the rocks after the explosion. She had seen, as he had, that Coronado was not among the pursuers, and she had gone back to find him.

"Damn her torn and twisted ideas," Fargo swore aloud as he sent the Ovaro up into the rocks and tried to find her trail. But there were too many prints, the rocky terrain too difficult to read, and he sent the Ovaro back toward the forest and the Mescalero camp. He passed cluster after cluster of torn, lifeless bodies. The dynamite had been effective, a substitute for a platoon of cavalry, just as he'd hoped it would be. He searched for a sign of Donna through the carnage and found none. He slowed when once again he came in sight of the camp.

The dynamite had done its work there with equal effectiveness. He saw the teepees hanging in shreds, most of the wickiups reduced to piles of kindling. Slain Mescalero littered the ground and a few braves helped a handful of squaws sift through the debris. The exploding shells had taken their own toll of victims, he realized, an altogether fitting answer to the slaughter on the plain. But Donna was not among those at the camp. He turned away, rode slowly through the early light, searching the forest. Finally he emerged back onto the rocks of the foothills.

It was a useless task to keep on searching, he realized. She could have gone anywhere, perhaps even followed Coronado. But he waited when he reached the flat land, positioning himself in the open where she could see him from the hills. He let the sun reach the noon sky and felt the burning of it before he finally turned and slowly began the ride east to Dry

Lake and the fort. He had done what he'd come to do. Perhaps he couldn't have saved Donna Honegger. She had at least partly atoned for her father's stupidity and ambition. He had sent a hundred young men to their deaths. She had helped stop the massacre of hundreds of settlers before it had a chance to begin. It seemed to even itself out, only it didn't really. It would have all been unnecessary if Danton Honegger had listened. Everything else was a price nobody need ever have paid.

Fargo spat, his mouth dry. Stupidity never evened out. It always carried too high a price tag and Donna was the last of it, driven by her own torn and twisted guilt. He carried the sourness in his mouth as he rode across the hot, dry flat land. He had left the high rock formations in the distance and knew he was halfway back to town when he glimpsed the movement through the haze of heat. He halted, watched, and movement became a horse and rider and the shimmering heat waves parted as the rider drew closer and Fargo saw the hawk-nose face and the slitted eyes.

He also saw the dry-wheat hair hanging down from the figure draped across the Mescalero pony's back. The Indian rode steadily toward him and Fargo turned the Ovaro around to face the man, his hand resting on the Colt at his side. Coronado halted a dozen paces away and flung Donna to the ground. With a rush of gratefulness, Fargo saw her lift herself up as the Indian sprang from the pony and grabbed her from behind. He held a long-bladed trapper's knife to Donna's throat and his eyes stayed on the big man in front of him. He spoke in Spanish, nodded with his head, but he could have spoken in

Apache dialect, his meaning unmistakable. Fargo unstrapped the gun belt as he slid from the Ovaro.

The Indian waited, the knife pressed a fraction deeper against Donna's throat. Fargo flung the gun belt with the Colt so that it landed at least a dozen yards away. Coronado stepped back, took the knife from Donna's throat. He smashed his fist into the small of Donna's back and with a gasped cry of pain she collapsed facedown on the ground.

The Indian stepped over her and came toward him. Fargo gathered his muscles as Coronado neared, the long-bladed knife upraised in one hand. Fargo feinted and the Indian lunged. Fargo sidestepped and brought a looping blow up that grazed Coronado's face. Eyes shining like black coals of hate, the Mescalero came at him again, the knife ready to strike. Fargo tried another feint and again the Indian lunged. This time Fargo's blow landed against the man's jaw and Coronado stumbled sideways. Fargo started in after him but the Mescalero chief was quick and he whirled, slashed, and Fargo felt the rush of air along his arm as the knife flashed by.

He backed away as Coronado slashed again. He tried a left hook that the Indian took in the ribs without a sound. But the blow hand landed and Fargo circled, took better aim, and came in again with another left hook, this one smashing into Coronado's midsection. Again, the man took the blow without a sound. Fargo weaved and threw a hard right. But Coronado didn't let this blow land. Instead, he arched downward with the trapper's knife and Fargo felt the sharp pain shoot through his arm as the knife slashed into him. The Trailsman fell backward, Mescalero leaping after him, slashing with quick, deft motions. Fargo fell back again, circled, and the Indian stayed with him. He had been suckered into a moment of false confidence, Fargo realized, and he cursed at himself as he felt the blood trickling down his arm. It was a game two could play, he vowed, and he stayed still as Coronado sliced with the knife again. The blade came close and Fargo went backward, seemed to stumble, and again Coronado's knife sliced within a fraction of an inch. Fargo let fear show in his face as he continued to go back and each slash of the knife came a fraction of an inch closer.

Fargo kept circling backward and saw the confidence in Coronado's face. The Indian rushed, sliced, and sliced again. Fargo tried a weak left and the Mescalero brushed it aside. He tried another with the same results and fell back again at Coronado's slice. He tried to turn, stumbled, let himself go, and fell half on his back. Coronado charged forward, the blade raised to kill. Fargo half-turned, seemed to be trying to twist away from the death-dealing blow. But as Coronado leapt forward, Fargo's leg kicked out and his foot caught the Mescalero in the groin. With a course grunt of pain, the Indian fell sideways to the ground and Fargo twisted and brought around a blow that landed on the Mescalero's temple.

Coronado rolled onto his side but he still clung to the knife and he managed to slash out in a backward swipe as Fargo came at him. Fargo had to fling himself backward and he stumbled—no sham this time— fell forward and heard the Mescalero come at him with the knife blade held spear-like in front of him. Coronado drove the blade forward and Fargo barely managed to keep the knife from ripping into his throat as he twisted his head to the side. He felt the blade slam into the dry ground and he managed to

159

bring his knees up and send Coronado almost somersaulting over his head. The Indian hit the ground hard and Fargo saw the blade fall from his hand. He dived for it where it lay on the ground and expected Coronado to do the same. He closed his hand around the knife and half-turned just in time to see the rock slam into his face. It hit him high on the temple and flashing lights exploded in his head as he fell back. Dimly, he realized the Indian had been able to scoop up one of the loose stones that dotted the flat land, most of them small but with sharp edges. He tried to clear his head, roll, but felt the rock slam into him again, this time along the back of his head.

He flung himself forward in a half-dive, half-roll. The flashing lights went off again, but he continued to roll and shook his head clear just in time to see the Mescalero over him, his hand coming down with the rock in it. Fargo managed to bring one knee up and it hit against Coronado's thigh with enough force to make the man's blow miss slamming into his face. Instead, it landed against his temple and the flashing lights filled his head again. He tried to fight off unconsciousness, rolled, shook his head, and cleared away enough grayness to see Coronado had raced back to retrieve the knife.

Fargo tried to turn, but his legs refused to respond. His head ached and he had to keep shaking it to stay conscious. He saw the Mescalero chief come over him, the knife blade raised to plunge it down into him in a final, killing blow. Fargo felt the grayness descending over him again and shook his head clear, but his arms and legs still seemed to be made of lead. He started to raise one arm and knew the motion was much too slow. He saw the Mescalero tighten his shoulder and arm muscles to plunge the blade downward when the shot rang out—a sharp, explosive sound in the vast, flat land. Coronado stiffened and Fargo saw the gusher of red burst through a hole that appeared in his abdomen. The Indian staggered, turned, the knife blade still upraised, and Fargo managed to lift his head enough to see Donna, the Colt in her hand. She had crawled to the gun belt while the battle raged, and now, both hands holding the gun up in front of her, she pulled the trigger again.

Coronado let out a final roar as his back ran red but with a last moment of fury he flung the knife with his last remaining bit of strength as he pitched forward. Fargo heard himself hiss as he saw the knife slam into Donna, embedding itself to the hilt just below her neck. She shivered in place for a moment and then her arms dropped and the gun fell from her hands. She collapsed on the spot, and Fargo, his head throbbing fiercely, slowly pulled himself to his feet. He half-stumbled his way to her where she lay. He fell on one knee beside her and lifted her face up.

He started to pull the knife from her and stopped. There was nothing to be gained by it except a flood of red. Donna Honegger opened her eyes, managed to focus on him. "Why didn't you stay with me, dammit?" he murmured. "You didn't have to do this."

"One last collision course," she breathed before her eyes closed, and he saw the wry smile touch her lips. He held her for a long time before he pulled himself to his feet and carried her gently to the Indian pony. He draped her over the pony's back and retrieved his gun belt. He rode slowly, very slowly, across the hot, silent territory and the day was almost at an end when he reached the fort leading the pony behind him.

Lieutenant Ridder came out and Fargo saw Ellie hurry to the gate from town as he slid from the horse and gave the reins of the pony to the lieutenant. "A proper burial, soldier," he said. "With a rifle salute, everything the way you'd do for the major."

"Yes, sir," the trooper said, and saluted.

Fargo saw the question still in his eyes. "It's over," he said. "There'll be no rampaging, not for a while. You'll have plenty of time to bring in replacements." He turned away and Ellie came to him, her hand folding around his arm as she walked down the main street with him.

"You can tell me tomorrow," she said. "Tonight we'll make you forget everything but making love."

"I'll sure try, honey. You can count on it." He smiled as he drew her warmth against him. "You'll have a story that'll win you a prize."

"I've won that," Ellie said as they reached the hotel and her mouth found his.

"Guess I have, too," he murmured, and pushed the door closed.

LOOKING FORWARD!

**The following is the opening
section from the next novel in the exciting
Trailsman series from Signet:**

THE TRAILSMAN #83
DEAD MAN'S FOREST

*The Utah Territory, 1860,
just east of Devil's Slide,
a land where law was more shadow
than substance . . .*

"You know who that woman is in bed with you, mister?"

Skye Fargo frowned as he stared up at the two men standing at the foot of the bed, each pointing a Remington .44 Army revolver at him. "Answer me, mister," the voice rasped and Fargo blinked as the question revolved inside his head again. He turned to stare at the woman lying a few inches from him in the big bed and took in a fleshy figure, almost flabby in its voluminous nakedness. Large breasts with more size than shape, a round belly, and fatty thighs were all topped by frizzled red hair atop a wide face.

Fargo turned his face back to the two men. "No, I don't know who she is or how the hell she got there," he said. "But I sure as hell never picked her out."

"She's my wife, that's who she is, Mister Fargo."
Fargo blinked again, fought the dull throbbing inside his

head, and stared at the man. Recognition slowly slid across his mind.

"You're the damn mayor, Efran Eason," he murmured.

"That's right," his accuser said. "And I could shoot you right there for having my wife in bed with you."

Fargo continued to stare at the man as he pushed himself up onto his elbows, glanced down at his own nakedness, and moved one hand toward the gunbelt hanging on the bedpost. "Keep away from that," the other man said. Fargo's lake-blue eyes peered at him. Recognition again pushed its way slowly across his mind.

"Sheriff Sideman," Fargo muttered and remembered the man's small, shifty eyes, his short nose, and tight mouth. Under close-cut black hair Sheriff Sideman had the face of a man who sought a quick dollar the way a ferret seeks a mole.

"Now that we all recognize each other you can get dressed, Fargo," the sheriff said. "I'm taking you to jail on Mayor Eason's charge."

Fargo glanced at the woman alongside him. She hadn't covered up any and he smiled grimly to himself. The immodesty made its own statement, and he let his eyes move over her body again. She had a purplish birthmark about the size of a copper penny on the side of her left thigh and on her left wrist she wore a narrow bracelet with initial *S* dangling from it. He'd seen that before, he frowned, or something like it. But he sure had never seen her before. He returned his eyes to the two men. Sideman stepped to the bedpost and removed the gunbelt with the big Colt in it.

Skye Fargo swung his long legs over one side of the bed, the muscles of his powerful body rippling, and started to pull on clothes. He glanced at Efran Eason and back at the woman still on the bed. "What's the charge, Sheriff? Doing a good deed?" he asked.

"Don't get smart, mister" the sheriff growled. "Taking another man's wife is a hanging offense around here."

"I never saw her before and you goddamn well know it," Fargo said calmly, glancing at the woman again as she rose and began to pull a slip over a more than ample rear.

"I doubt that Judge Hibbs will believe that," the sheriff said. Fargo ignored the statement and realized that he remembered little of last night after he'd gone to the dance hall. Not because he'd drunk himself into a stupor. He'd only had one drink. He remembered that clearly enough, and he eyed the two men as they motioned him toward the door of the room with their guns. He felt the anger gathering inside him as he pulled the door open to steip into a corridor with Sherifff Sideman close behind him.

"Keep walking," the sheriff said. Fargo moved down the hallway and past the front desk of what was plainly the town hotel. When he was marched outside, he saw his horse hitched there, the striking black-and-white Ovaro unmistakable, and he felt a moment of surprise. He let a grim sound escape his lips. They were being neat. They'd brought the Ovaro there just as they'd brought him to the hotel.

He had been set up, Fargo realized, starting with that single drink he'd been served at the dance hall, a drink that had obviously been doctored to drug him. He remembered little after that lone drink, but putting the rest together was easy enough. The grim anger still inside him, he saw the woman leave the hotel, a shawl around her. She began to hurry away and Fargo glimpsed the narrow bracelet again, the initial dangling from it. It was still somehow familiar, but he couldn't pin it down. His head was still fuzzy and throbbing, he realized; he needed more time to let the drug wear off completely before he began to put the pieces together. But the picture was slowly taking form. He glanced at Efran Eason's short figure. "Aren't you going to see the little wifey home, Mayor?" he asked.

"Of course I am," tha man said. He tried to look righteously angry but secceeded only in appearing petulant. Eason was the kind of man who went through life like a toad, Fargo decided, forever ready to hop in any direction. The sheriff prodded him in the back with his Remington, and Fargo moved forward, his eyes taking in the still, dark town in the small hours of the morning. The town had a name, Hardrock, but it was a good deal more prosperous than many small towns in the territory. It had the usual dance hall, and muddy main street, but it also boasted a bank, a church, and a schoolhouse at the north end of town. Hardrock, he'd come to see in the few days he'd been there, sat in a perfect place in the northeast corner of Utah. Those journeying west passed through to avoid the Unita Mountains and those coming down from Wyoming could pause here before going on in any direction. Its location let Hardrock serve those settlers who put down roots in the territory and those passing through to somewhere else. That allowed it to combine a certain air of respectability with the rowdy and raucous nature of most such towns. He'd even seen a converted grain shed made into a way station for, as the sign said, the followers of Brigham Young.

But Hardrock had been a good choice for Molly to make a fresh start, and it had been Molly Mason that had brought him here. He half smiled and cast a glance at Sheriff Sideman walking close behind him. "All this shit wouldn't have anything to do with our little talk the other day, would it?" he offered.

"Not a damn thing. You were caught with Mayor Eason's wife in bed. It's as simple as that."

"The hell it is," Fargo laughed. He followed the sheriff's gesture as he motioned to a narrow building with a star on the window. Fargo opened the door and went inside, where a barred cell took up the back half of the room with a smaller cell to one side and a desk and gun cabinet in the front of the space. The sheriff pushed him into the larger cell and slammed the door shut. Fargo turned around, grimaced as a sharp throb stabbed through his head. Sheriff Sideman surveyed him from outside the bars for a long moment.

"Of course, if you want to talk about not staying in jail I might be able to persuade the mayor to be forgiving," the sheriff said.

Fargo allowed a slow smile. "According to him, his wife wound up in bed with me. Hell, I'm the one who ought to be forgiving." Fargo saw the Sheriff's eyes harden.

"Sleep on it, Fargo. That's advice I'd take," Sheriff Sideman growled.

"Sure thing," Fargo said. He sat down on the narrow cot that took up one part of the wall. He saw a cracked white porcelain pitcher of water and an open toilet in the other corner of the cell. He waited until the sheriff stalked from the office and slammed the front door after him before he lay back and stretched out on the cot, his long legs dangling from one end. A small smile touched his lips. Their little scheme was really very transparent, but he needed to put all the pieces into place from the beginning. He had to be certain he was right before they came again. He closed his eyes and let his mind unwind, travel backwards to when he had arrived in Hardrock. And why.

It had been only a few days back, the moment he'd finished bringing in Bill Dempster's herd. He'd taken the long, hard drive only because it ended at Hardrock, and it gave him a chance to keep a promise made long ago. Molly's letters had told him she worked at the general store, and she and Amy lived in a white cottage just past town. He had arrived late in the day, found the cottage and Molly. "Oh, my God, I'm dreaming," she had gasped before flying into his arms, her lips quickly finding his.

"You look wonderful, Molly," he said when he pulled back. "As bright and sunny as always." No mere words on his part, for Molly Mason's dark hair and snapping black-brown eyes always reflected the brightness that was inside her, a quality that saw her through trials and troubles without turning her bitter. She had taken her arms from around his neck as the little girl appeared behind her, the same darkly bright eyes and deep-brown hair.

"This is an old friend, Amy," Molly introduced. "He remembers when you were born back in Kansas six years ago."

"He sure does," Fargo echoed and drew a shy smile from little Amy. He had dinner with Molly and her daughter, and after Amy was in bed and asleep, Molly took him into her room and her lips found his again.

"I've never forgotten how you helped me after Chuck was killed," she said. "And that wonderful year after Amy was born when you'd stay with me after every trip."

"Seems long ago, doesn't it?" he had remarked.

"Too long," Molly had said. "But you've finally come and it's time to replacing dreaming with doing." She had turned her words into action as with a wriggle of her shoulder she let the nightgown drop away. Time had done nothing to diminish the lovely curve of her full breasts, he saw. Their dark pink points were already firm with desire. He started to pull off his clothes, but Molly stopped him. "Let me," she breathed. She began to undress him, pausing to caress and kiss and rub against him after each garment pulled away. When he was finally naked, his powerfully muscled body against her, Molly Mason uttered a deep and groaning sigh as he began to make love to her. She responded with hunger and memories, everything wrapped and entwined together, as their bodies quickly melded. Molly's full-curved loveliness clung to him, and the clock turned back with every soft scream of her pleasure. When she rose up in climax her thighs encased him with sweet quivering.

Later, stretched out against him, Molly nuzzled into his chest. "How long can you stay, Skye?" she asked.

"Long enough," he said. "Been on the trail too much. Came here to see you and do nothing else."

"Wonderful," Molly had murmured. But we'll have to be a little more discreet than we used to be. I've a daughter and a job, and I'm a respected member of the community.

"You call the shots, honey."

"Same time, same place tomorrow night," Molly had laughed as she wrapped one leg over his and went to sleep in his arms. He left in the morning before little Amy awoke and decided to pay the town barber a visit. It was when he left the barber shop that he found the two men standing beside the Ovaro.

"Fargo?" the one man said and went on without waiting for an answer. "Been looking for you. Bill Dempster told us you rode an extra fine Ovaro. I'm Sheriff Sideman. This is our mayor, Efran Eason." Fargo nodded and felt a touch of wariness stab at him. "We've been waiting for you to arrive with Dempster's herd. He told us you were due soon." Fargo felt the wariness grow stronger inside him and waited. "We've a special job for you, Fargo," the sheriff said. "We need you to trail a man for us."

"Sorry, you'll have to get somebody else," Fargo said.

"I'm tired, I'm trail-weary and I'm taking a good long rest."

"We need the very best and that's you. We'll pay you twice your usual fee," the mayor had said.

Fargo smiled pleasantly. "Sorry, but not this time around, gents."

"Three times your usual fee," Efran Eason offered.

"This hombre must be real important to you," Fargo commented.

"He's a very dangerous man and we want him back dead or alive. That's why we need you," the mayor said.

"He got a name?" Fargo asked.

"Frank Tupper," the sheriff answered.

"He a specially good woodsman or mountain man?" Fargo queired.

"No, but time's very important. We need someone who can pick up his trail and catch him before he gets too far away," the sheriff put in.

"What'd he do?" Fargo asked out of curiousity.

"He cleaned out the town treasury, most of the money in the bank, and killed two tellers; Sideman answered.

"Just the same, you'll have to find somebody else, I'm afraid," Fargo said. "I don't usually turn down good money, but this is a special time and a special visit here. Sorry."

We can't accept that, Fargo," the sheriff said, his voice hardening. "This is too important to us. We need him caught and we know you're the only man who can do it."

" 'Fraid you'll have to accept it, gents," Fargo said pleasantly. He ignored the glowering frowns as he swung onto the Ovaro. Their eyes bored into him as he rode away.

That night he returned to Molly and once again, after Amy was asleep, she came with all her eager warmth, and the night became a thing of sweet touchings and throbbing tenderness until he lay with her in the warm aftermath of ecstacy. Once again, when morning came, he left before little Amy woke and it was later in the day when, Efran Eason and the sheriff approached him. He had stopped at the smithy to have the Ovaro's right foreshoe tightened, and the two men appeared with a third man who joined them on horseback. Fargo took in the man in the saddle and saw sand-colored hair cut very short, a square face with a pushed-in nose, and a mouth that turned down at the corners. It was a face as harsh as a granite quarry.

"This is Olson, Fargo," Sideman said. "He's a kind-of deputy for me."

"Whatever that means," Frago remarked.

"It means he does special jobs for me when I need him," the sheriff said. Olson stared down from the saddle, his harsh face unsmiling. He had brought the horse alongside a deep water trough, Fargo saw. "We still need you on that job, Fargo," the sheriff pressed.

"The answer's still no," Fargo returned. He let the annoyance show in his voice now.

"You're obviously enjoying your visit to Hardrock," Sheriff Sideman said. Fargo's eyes grew narrow.

"What's that mean?" he questioned.

"Miss Mason is a lovely young woman, a welcome part of our community," Efran Eason said.

"You've been following me," Fargo muttered, steel coming into his voice.

"Just to be sure you don't leave town without considering our offer again," the mayor said.

"I don't like being watched. It makes me very irritable and things happen when I get irritable," Fargo growled. "I'm not taking your damn job, so get off my back."

Olson's voice cut in, a harsh, grating sound to it. "Hell, he's more interested in tail than trail," the man said.

Excerpt from DEAD MAN'S FOREST

Fargo stood very still for a moment. When his hand lashed out, it was with the speed of a rattler's strike and he closed his fingers around Olson's belt buckle. He yanked, all the strength of his powerful shoulder muscles behind it, and Olson came forward from his horse. Fargo twisted and the man landed headfirst into the water trough with a loud and wet splash. Fargo, his grip loosened, stepped back and then forward, pushing Olson's head deeper into the water.

"Let him go. You're drowning him, dammit," he heard the sheriff say and saw the man reach for his sixgun.

"You draw and you can be sure I'll drown him," Fargo said, and the sheriff lowered his hand. Fargo waited another ten seconds and then yanked Olson up from the trough. The man came up coughing and spitting water between deep, heaving breaths. Fargo half twisted him around in the trough and drove his forearm against the man's throat, Olson's head pressed against the edge of the trough. "Molly Mason's an old friend of mine. You call her tail again and I'll break your damn neck, you hear me?" Fargo rasped. Olson made a gasping sound that sufficed as a yes, and Fargo let him go and stepped back. He turned to Efran Eason and the sheriff while Olson lay in the rough regaining his breath, his head just above water. "I make myself clear to you gents?" Fargo growled. The sheriff's face showed he was a man who knew when to let caution rule over anger. Efran Eason showed only fear. He quickly turned and walked away with Sideman. Fargo waited till Olson pulled himself from the trough and led his horse away.

The smithy was waiting with the Ovaro, and Fargo swung onto the horse and rode from town. Efran Eason and his sheriff were two worried and persistent men, but perhaps they'd learned their lesson finally, Fargo hoped.

He didn't return to Molly's place till after dark. His eyes searched the streets as he neared the cottage, but he spied no shadowy figures. Once he was inside, Molly pressed her lips to his and finally pulled away with dismay wreathing her face.

"Amy's sick. She's in her room," Molly told him. "She's running a fever. I'm afraid I'll be sitting up with her through the night."

"Anything you need?" Fargo asked.

"No, I'll call Doc Grogan if she's not better come morning," Molly said.

He cupped her face in one hand. "I'm sorry for Amy and disappointed for me," he said.

"That makes two of us," Molly said as she leaned into his chest.

"See you tomorrow night," he told her. He patted her soft bottom as she kissed him at the door and went back into the night. He was hungry and decided a drink and something to eat would be perfect. He had walked the Ovaro to the dance hall, tethered the horse to the post outside, and gone into a round and smoky room, a curved bar taking up one side. His glance halted at the woman in the tight blue dress. She was pushing forty, he guessed. It was wasy to recognize the granite-faced man beside her. Olson's eyes found him and the man turned his back to Fargo as he continued talking to the woman. Fargo strolled to one of the small table beside the wall, eased his big frame into the small, straight-backed chair, and one of the house girls in a short frock and black net stocking came over. They all wore pretty much the same outfit, he noted. The girl, still young but with too much makeup around her eyes, regarded him with a bored appraisal.

"What's your pleasure, big man?" she had said. "Pour, plate, or pillow?"

"We'll start with pour. Bourbon," he'd laughed and

watched her wend her way through the crowded room. Two of the other dance hall girls crossed his line of vision, and he watched them idly, one almost skinny, the other almost fat and neither particularly pretty. The girl took a ridiculously long time to return with his bourbon, he remembered now and she'd hurried away without another word. Not that he cared at the time. He'd been happy to relax and slowly sip the drink.

Fargo stretched his neck muscles as his thoughts clicked off. He had come to the end of his rememberings. Now he had to piece together what happened afterward, not that it was terribly hard to do. Olson had seen an opportunity to get back at him and arranged to have the bourbon doctored. Then he'd reported what he'd done to his boss. The sheriff had undoubtedly called in Efran Eason, and the rest of the scheme was cooked up. It was really quite transparent, all of it an attempt to make him agree to trail for them.

But they'd made themselves a mistake, Fargo grunted. He'd let them go through all the motions until they came to realize it wouldn't work. He let his mind wander some more, and the woman in the bed next to him swam into his thoughts. he frowned as he thought about the narrow bracelet with the initial dangling from it. It continued to seem familiar. Suddenly he sat up and a half laugh, half snort fell from his lips. The girl that had brought him the bourbon had worn one with her initial dangling from it. So had the other two girls, he recalled. It was a kind of house trademark, apparently, and Fargo smiled as he lay back on the cot. He'd been sure she hadn't been the mayor's wife, but now he knew where they'd gotten her. From the dance hall, he laughed. That explained her lack of modesty. She was used to lying naked before strangers. They had put together a neat package, Fargo pondered. There had to be another link, something yet to come to add the final finish. The judge, he laughed. They had to have a judge to complete the picture and make him think he was in deep trouble.

Fargo smiled, pushed himself up farther on the cot, and closed his eyes. Sleep seemed the best idea at the moment, and he turned on his side and drew slumber around him at once. The cell remained a quiet place through the night, and when daylight came in through the lone window he rose, used the porcelain pitcher of water to wash and freshen himself. He'd just finished when the front door opened. Sheriff Sideman entered first, Efran Eason behind him, and the last figure a tall, lanky, long-faced man with graying hair and the face of a pious, backwoods preacher. But the man wore a black frock coat, a wing collar, and a diamond stickpin in a blue cravat.

Fargo eyed the man with amusement. "You must be the judge," he said and saw the man's pale gray eyes widen in surprise.

"I didn't expect to be expected," the man said with a glance at Efran Eason.

"I'm good at figuring out things," Fargo remarked casually.

"I have no idea what that means, sir," the man said. "I'm Judge Warren Hibbs and Mayor Eason asked me to stop in and explain the seriousness of the charges against you."

"That's real nice of you, Judge," Fargo said blandly.

"Forcing another man's wife to bed is a serious thing. I'd have to sentence you to hang if you're found guilty," Judge Hibbs said gravely.

"What about the mayor's good wife? It takes two to tango," Fargo remarked.

"I understand Mrs. Eason says you seized her on the street and forced her into the hotel room with you," the judge said.

"Only it was the other way around. She did the forcing," Fargo said.

"That hardly seems likely," the Judge said.

"You didn't see her naked," Fargo said. "I feel sorry for the good mayor."

"Dammit, Fargo, this isn't some game," Efran Eason interrupted angrily.

"You could've fooled me," Fargo said.

"The judge came down here to help you help yourself," Eason insisted.

"He's got a heart of gold. You all do." Fargo smiled.

Judge Hibbs exchanged a quick glance with Efran Eason and returned his eyes to the big man on the other side of the bars. "You seem determined to meet under more formal conditions, Mister Fargo," he said, his lips pursed.

Fargo shrugged. "It'll be her word against mine," he said. The judge turned on his heel and strode from the building, a thin, lanky form followed by the mayor's short portly figure and Sheriff Sideman bringing up in the rear like two crows following a crane.

Fargo returned to the cot. Eason and the sheriff knew by now that he was onto what they were trying to do, but he wondered about Judge Hibbs. Had the judge simply been doing his friends a favor, or did he have more of a part in it? Only one thing was unmistakably clear. Eason and the sheriff both wanted Frank Tupper back with a desperation that seemed more personal than just the pursuit of a thief and a killer. Yet perhaps they were both simply vengeful, as well as zealous defenders of the town's interests. He wondered how much further they'd try to carry on with their charade before giving up on him. He stretched out and closed his eyes to wait.